THE SPYBRARIAN

Jon Mayhew

THE SPYBRARIAN

JON MAYHEW

uclanpublishing

The *Spybrarian* is a uclanpublishing book

First published in Great Britain in 2020 by
uclanpublishing
University of Central Lancashire
Preston, PR1 2HE, UK

978-1-9129793-5-6

1 3 5 7 9 10 8 6 4 2

Set in 10/17pt Kingfisher by Toni Murtagh

A CIP catalogue record for this book is available from the British Library.

Printed and bound in Great Britain by Clays Ltd, Elcograf S.p.A.

In memory of
Tommy Donbavand

Friend
Mentor
Genius

"READ IT OR THE BATTLE HAMSTERS
WILL NIBBLE YOUR BUM!"

MARK POWERS

WHAT DO WE WANT?
WHEN DO WE WANT IT?

I *wish aliens would come and kidnap me,* **RIGHT NOW,** *I thought.*
Or maybe a big hole could open up and I'd fall **SCREAMING TO**
MY DEATH. *Or a* **GIANT SEAGULL** *could swoop down and take*
me high in the sky. If any of those things had happened, I was
pretty sure that one day, people would say, "Remember that
Kian Reader, you know the lad who was snatched from the street
by a giant seagull? I'll never forget that." Right now, I was pretty
sure I'd be remembered as the "lad whose mum's new boyfriend
DRESSED UP AS THE GRUFFALO and made a **HOLY SHOW** of himself
outside the Town Hall." There was a small crowd of people
but they were all dressed sensibly in coats and woolly hats.

1

Only Anthony, Mum's New Boyfriend, wore a huge, hairy brown suit with fangs and claws. So embarrassing.

Anthony wasn't happy with just dressing up as a character from a soppy kid's book. Oh no, he had also decided to carry a huge sign with 'I Love Libraries' painted on it and to shout out at the top of his voice, "What do we want?"

Then Mum joined in and I could feel myself shrivelling up on the pavement. "No Library closures!"

"When do we want them?"

"Now!" Mum yelled.

Actually, I thought, the best thing in the world right now would be if a stretch limo pulled up and a billionaire climbed out and told me there'd been a **BIG MIX-UP** at the hospital and I was really the billionaire's only son.

"What do we want, Kian?" Anthony bellowed over my head.

"To go home?" I muttered, feebly.

"When do we want it?"

"NOW!"

Mum leant close to my ear. "Come on, Kian, you know libraries are important. Anthony says that —"

"I don't care what Anthony says. He looks like a proper 'nana dressed up like that and libraries are boring. I hope they all close." The daft thing was, I actually had to go to the library before they closed at twelve o'clock! But here I was, wasting my Saturday morning standing outside the Town Hall with a

GROWN MAN IN A GRUFFALO ONESIE. I hated my life. Yesterday, Mr Vestibule, the new English teacher, had made an absolute fool of me in front of the whole class because I'd forgotten my homework.

Mr Vestibule was the **POLAR OPPOSITE** of me. That means very opposite to me, it doesn't mean that he was from the North Pole or anything. Come to think of it, he was very cold towards me so . . . who knows? What I meant was that he was old, I was young. He was tall, I was short. He was round, I was skinny. He was bald, I had lots of mousy brown hair that covered my eyes and ears.

Plus, Mr Vestibule had a **LOOOOOOOONG** pointy nose and massively **WIDE** nostrils full of bristly hairs and if you got too close you could see right up them. If you were **REALLY, REALLY** unlucky, you'd catch a glimpse of some bogeys clinging to the bristles. I don't know if my nose is that bristly or snotty because I've got better things to do than get a mirror and try to look up my own nose. I hope my nose isn't that hairy.

"You forgot!" Mr Vestibule said again, as if I had just jumped out of my seat, run around the class yodelling and smeared dog poo all over the whiteboard. "You forgot your reading log?"

"Yes, sir, sorry sir," I said, as innocently as possible. Truth was, I'd just not done it. I hate reading. It's boring.

Mr Vestibule looked around at the class. It was like a signal to the rest of the class that the ritual humiliation was about

3

to begin. "Did you forget to *GET DRESSED* this morning?"

Everyone chuckled. Almost everyone. Prissy McBeef sat scowling at the top of her biro in the corner of the room but I wasn't sure why.

"No, sir," I muttered, looking down at my hands.

"Did you forget your *BREAKFAST*, this morning?"

Everyone chuckled again, even Velcro Asif and he was meant to be my best friend. I decided we'd have words about that later.

"No, sir," I said.

"Did you forget to *GO TO THE TOILET*, this morning?"

The whole class was laughing now and even Mr Vestibule gave a tight smile. I flashed a look at Velcro who grinned an apology back then straightened his face.

"No, sir," I said.

"No sir," Mr Vestibule repeated, and took a deep breath. "You've been at St Jeffery of the Immaculate Hot Cross Bun Middle School for only four weeks and already, you're slipping into bad habits . . ." Apparently hundreds of years ago, Hinderton had been *HIT BY THE PLAGUE* and Saint Jeff had fed the *ENTIRE* population of the town with *ONE HOT CROSS BUN*. That was why he became a saint and our school got the daftest name in the country.

"I know, sir, sorry, sir," I said again.

"Very well," Mr Vestibule said. "I want that reading log first thing on Monday and you will go to the local library this weekend to get a particular book out. Do you know what the title of the book is, Kian?"

"No, sir."

Mr Vestibule gave a nasty grin. "*Improve Your Memory Skills*," he said. Everyone gave a murmur of wonder. You had to hand it to him. It was a REALLY CRAFTY PUNISHMENT because it used up your time without Mr Vestibule having to do anything and sometimes it even used up your parents' time and you'd get into trouble twice. Once with Mr Vestibule and then once with your parents for messing them about. "Bring me the book and your reading log on Monday without fail. Or else!"

"Kian!" Mum said, snapping me out of my daydream, or should I say, my DAYNIGHTMARE? I looked up at Mum. "Pay attention, look! The Mayor has just come out to talk to us all."

A lady with a huge cloud of blonde hair on her head and a thick gold chain around her shoulders stood on a wooden platform, ready to speak into a microphone. But I wasn't really looking at the mayor, I had my eye on the men behind her. One was incredibly tall and thin, wearing a long, black leather coat and a weird, wide-brimmed hat. The other was … MR VESTIBULE and he was staring right at me!

The Mayor tapped the microphone and it gave a sad whine. "I understand that many of you are concerned at the proposed library closures …"

Everyone booed. Anthony shook his placard. "Shame on

you!" He yelled. I just kept my head down but I could tell Mr Vestibule was glaring at me. I could feel his eyes drilling a hole in the top of my head! What was he doing here anyway? And why was he standing behind the mayor?

"It's not something I like doing... but unless the Government ... give more to local councils, then we simply can't afford to pay for them," the mayor continued. She looked a bit wide-eyed and her words sounded a bit mechanical. Why was she speaking like a robot? "Rest assured that the central library will still be open and will have a one-stop shop, plenty of computers to access the internet..."

"What about picture books?" Anthony yelled, shaking his placard again. "What about fiction?"

"Our volunteers will be able to help you find any kind of book you require and, of course, there is the internet..."

"Why do you keep going on about the internet?" Anthony shouted. "We need real books on real bookshelves..."

I could feel myself not just DYING WITH EMBARRASSMENT but also SHRIVELLING under the SCORCHING gaze of Mr Vestibule. I turned to Mum. "Mum, I've got to go. I've just remembered that I have to get a book from the library!"

Mum blinked at me. "There won't be a library if we don't make a stand," she said.

"Please Mum, it's for homework. I'll get into trouble if I don't go now and they close at twelve."

Anthony grinned at me. "Go on then, sport, Hinderton Central's just over there.

I glowered at Anthony. He thought I just wanted to get away, but I wanted to get Mr Vestibule's book AND get away from Mr Vestibule AND get away from Anthony! "Erm, the book I need is only at the branch library. You know the one by our house?"

Mum pursed her lips. "Why didn't you say before we came out? Go on then, we'll meet you back at home."

"Thanks," I said and ran off, leaving Mr Vestibule's EVIL glare far behind. It was only as I ran down the street that I remembered that I'd thrown my library card away last week. Anthony had been going on about how great reading was and how it changed his life. I dumped my card in the bin on the way to school that morning. If I was going to get the book, I was going to have to steal it!

THE GREAT LIBRARY ROBBERY

By the time I got to the branch library, it was almost twelve and the place had emptied out. It was a funny little square building that reminded me of a lunch box. The rows of books in the library glared at me and I glared back. **BOOKS REALLY ARE RUBBISH**, I thought. Only **LOSERS** read books.

I thought about Anthony in his Gruffalo suit and snorted. Dad, my *real* dad, didn't read books. He went **FISHING**. Right then, I wished I was sitting on the canal side with him, rather than crouching behind a bookcase in this stupid place.

The smell of the book covers mixed with floor polish, tickling my nose. A few low, comfy chairs lounged around beside the dark, wooden bookshelves. The hum of the traffic outside seemed miles away.

The librarian stood at the counter, the light reflecting off her pointy glasses. Her grey hair was all spiked up on top of her head and two dangly earrings swung back and forth as she glanced from one book to another. A gold bracelet rattled on her skinny wrist as she plonked a pile of World Record books on the smooth surface. I had to admit, the bright red, checked suit she wore made her look kind of cool. Like a retired rock star. But she was *ancient*! Older even than Mrs Jefferson who lived opposite us and threw digestives to the pigeons in Hinderton Town Square.

She probably wouldn't even notice if I grabbed a book and ran for it, I thought. *Even if she did notice, she wouldn't be able to catch me.* There was nobody else in the library to stop me either. The old librarian picked up another pile of books and files. I noticed a small bottle of blue liquid on the top of the pile.

Improve Your Memory Skills sat waiting for me on the bookshelf. It was just as well, really, I couldn't have walked up to the old biddy at the counter and said, "Excuse me but I'm looking for a book to steal, yes, one about memory skills." I felt awful. I'm not in the habit of stealing things but I just couldn't bear the thought of Mr Vestibule tearing me off a strip on Monday. Plus he'd probably keep me in, too. There was no choice. Taking a deep breath, I reached for the book, ready to stuff it under my jacket and RUN FOR IT.

At that moment, the library door creaked open and in walked **MARTIN MARVELLO THE FAMOUS, LOCAL, BEST-SELLING, AWARD-WINNING CHILDREN'S AUTHOR.** I couldn't believe my eyes but it was him all right! He'd visited our primary school when I was in Year 6 and his picture was all over school for weeks. And there could be no mistaking the yellow trousers and jacket he always wore. He looked weird and walked like a robot or like he was sleepwalking.

The librarian stopped and frowned at Marvello. "Hello, Martin," she said, peering at him. "Are you all right?"

I ducked behind a bookcase and peered through a gap in the books at the two of them.

Martin Marvello pulled a gun from his pocket and pointed it at the librarian!

"I . . . must . . . kill . . . Paige . . . Turner," he said, in a weird voice. He sounded like he was repeating an order. It reminded me of the Mayor giving her speech.

The librarian blinked. "I beg your pardon?" she said.

"I . . . must . . . kill . . . Paige . . . Turner," he said again.

"Really, Martin! Guns are *not* allowed in the library!" The librarian said. "Put that *away!* Someone will get hurt, or worse, you might damage a book."

BAM! The gun shot went off and my eyes widened as, at the same time, the old lady ducked under the counter, dodging the bullet. Then, she popped up again. "Martin, this is no way for a famous, local, best-selling, award-winning children's author to behave!" she said, her voice really shrill now. "And mind the displays!"

BAM! She ducked again and then popped her head up once more.

"I'm warning you Martin," she said. "I'll take action if I have to!"

BAM! BAM! Bullets smacked into the varnished counter, sending splinters of wood everywhere.

"Right, that does it," the librarian snapped and, still holding the pile of books and the bottle, she leapt up, vaulting over the desk. She flew forwards, spinning twice, her dangly earrings rattling and a biro flying out of her suit pocket. "**HIIIIIIIIIYAAAAAAH!**" Her leg stretched out straight. She landed, spinning like a ballet dancer, and **WHAM!** planted a stunning roundhouse kick to the side of Martin Marvello's head. He staggered back into a display of picture books. The gun spun off into the air, landing safely in the large print section.

But as she had jumped, she had dropped the books and files she had been holding.

And the bottle.

The books tumbled left and right, smacking on the floor.

The files spun off into the corners of the library, sliding along the polished floor with a hiss.

And the bottle whirled high in the air. I watched it as if in slow motion. It was small and the fluorescent lights shimmered through the blue liquid contents reminding me of those advertisements for sunny Mediterranean holidays. Then things speeded up and the bottle described a perfect arc through the air towards me.

I *reached* up to catch it.

I *fumbled* as the glass slid through my fingers.

I *gasped* as the bottle shattered right on my forehead.

Stars splintered before my eyes and a warm, wet liquid stung my face, filling my nose and mouth, making me cough and splutter.

The liquid burnt my skin, the inside of my mouth, my nostrils. Even that funny little bit between my nose and top lip (what's that called then?).

I lay on my back staring up at the lights in the ceiling. Everything looked blue at first but slowly the stinging stopped and my sight returned to normal. I blinked and sat up.

Martin Marvello and the librarian were engaged in a **DEADLY MARTIAL ARTS FACE-OFF**. The librarian leapt high into the air and backflipped away from Martin Marvello's deadly kick. Then she landed and planted a powerful punch right on the author's nose.

POW!

Martin Marvello staggered backwards, crashing into a glass cabinet.

"Mind the local history display!" the librarian screamed and brought a karate blow down on his shoulder. "And how did you get so good at Kung-Fu, Martin?"

"Research for . . . my . . . bestselling . . . Ninja . . . Wallabies . . . Series . . . Die!" Martin Marvello said in his monotonous, robotic voice. He staggered towards her, his face bruised, his jacket torn at the shoulder.

The librarian stood squarely in front of him, brown shoes planted firmly on the ground. "I never liked those books. I much preferred War Gerbil," she said, blocking his blow and BURYING her right fist into his stomach.

"OOOOFFF!" He doubled up, gasping as the breath left his body. With a sharp left uppercut to his chin, the librarian put him onto the floor. Martin Marvello lay groaning but still.

With a puzzled frown and a grunt of dissatisfaction, the librarian, straightened her tweed suit. Then she turned and looked directly at me. "Are you all right?" she said. Then her eyes widened and her hand flew to her mouth. "Oh my word. Did the bottle hit you?"

I clambered to my feet. It hurt between my eyes where the bottle had hit me and I felt a bit dizzy but otherwise I felt all right. "Yes," I said. "It really stung but it's okay now."

The librarian looked from Martin Marvello to me and then back again. The famous, local, best-selling, award-winning children's author wasn't going anywhere. She turned to me and grabbed a book from the shelf close to him.

"Read this," she said.

"W-what?" I stammered. "No. I don't like reading...I..."

The librarian went pale. Small red spots appeared on her wrinkled cheeks. "Never mind all that nonsense young man. Just. Read."

I stared down at the open book. My head **SPUN** and then the words seemed to rush towards me. I felt as if I was going **UP IN AN ELEVATOR**. It felt like my brain had been put on fast-forward. Suddenly, I knew it was a book **ALL ABOUT HOW JET ENGINES WORK**. "The-compressed-air-is-then-sprayed-with-fuel-and..." I zoomed through the text. "Electric-spark-lights-the-mixture ... burning gases expand ... blast out through the nozzle, at the back..." I couldn't stop.

Finally, the librarian **SLAMMED** the book shut. I felt like I'd been dragged off a roundabout going at **SIXTY MILES AN HOUR**. I wobbled a little and she grabbed my arm to steady me.

I rubbed my head "What happened?" I said. "Why do I suddenly know how a jet engine works?"

The librarian just shook my hand. "My name's Paige Turner, SLS," she said. Martin Marvello started to rise but Paige Turner leapt over and gave him a sharp blow to the top of the head. "Welcome to the dangerous world of books!"

Chapter 3

372.4

IT'S ALL GONE DOG-EARED.

I stared at Paige Turner. "What's going on?" I said. "Who are the SLS?"

Paige Turner checked that nobody else was there to listen in. "The Secret Library Service," she hissed. "Who Reads Wins!"

"W-what? Like spies or Special forces," I stammered. "Only . . . you're librarians too?"

Paige Turner nodded. "Yes, a bit of both, I suppose," she said. "How do you feel?"

"A bit dizzy," I replied. "And I seem to know a lot of stuff about jet engines. What was in that bottle?"

Paige looked a bit shifty and a bit sad. "That," she sighed, "was the one and only sample of *Reader Serum*."

"Reader Serum?"

"A potion designed to give the superpowers of reading to the person who takes it," Paige said. "Super-fast reading, super comprehension, super inference . . ."

"It gave me superpowers?" I said, pulling a face.

Paige pursed her lips and grabbed another thick book. "Super *Reading* Powers. Here," she said. "Try this if you don't believe me."

I flicked through the pages of equations and complicated words and that feeling of rising in a lift and information zapping through my brain hit me once more. "Wow," I said. "I always thought Quantum Theory was a bit complicated but," I shrugged, "after reading that, it seems obvious!" And it was TRUE! At that moment, I could have explained it all, just like that! I felt super-brainy!

"You see? Not only do you read really fast but you understand EVERYTHING that you read. You just *know* it straight away. You're a SUPER READER!"

I blinked in disbelief and MY HEART THUMPED in excitement. "So if I read about Superman," I said, "then I'll have all his powers? Flight, laser eyes," I swallowed hard, "X-ray vision, even?"

Paige Turner rolled her eyes. "Of course not," she said. "It only works on non-fiction as far as we know. I wouldn't go trying to leap over any tall buildings in a single bound."

MY HEART SANK. "Brilliant, of all the super powers to get, I get *super reading powers!* Typical!" I muttered. "Why couldn't I have been bitten by a radioactive spider? Or been given the ability to fly?"

Paige shook her head and sighed. "The Reader Serum was developed by a brilliant brain surgeon, Professor Randolph von Gleitz," she said. "He was trying to cure dyslexia. Sadly, he died in an explosion in his lab. It destroyed all of his notes. Everything was lost apart from that last sample which he sent to me before the accident. All we knew was that there was enough in the sample for one young person."

I looked down on the unconscious author. "But why did *he* want to kill you?" "Hypnosis," Paige said.

"What?"

"I prefer 'pardon,' young man," Paige said. "I'm afraid that Martin Marvello the famous, local, best-selling, award-winning children's author was hypnotised into trying to kill me and stealing the serum."

"Hang on a minute," I said, getting more and more confused. "Who would want to kill you and steal this . . . serum thingy?"

"*Fart,*" Paige Turner said.

I blinked. "Wha . . . I mean, I beg your pardon."

"I said *Fart,*" Paige said again.

"What?" I glanced around, and my face reddened. "Here? Now?"

"No!" Paige said. "The Fellowship Against Reading Texts or F.A.R.T. for short. It's an evil, secret organisation that wants to stop people from reading and learning. They've been hypnotising all kinds of people all over the country and making them do all kinds of stupid things like closing libraries and sacking librarians. Hideous! They have the Mayor of Hinderton under their power and this library will close soon enough, if they get their way!"

I thought about the mayor giving her speech in her robot voice. The same kind of voice as Martin Marvello! "So, this evil organisation has hypnotised the mayor . . ."

"Ssh!" Paige said holding up her hand. "Do you feel that?"

I frowned. "What are you talking about?" I started to say but I stopped. There was something in the air. "It's weird. It feels like something is about to happen . . ."

"Like the tension's building . . ." Paige said.

I nodded. "Yes."

"Ellipsis missiles!" Paige yelled. "RUN!" She pushed me towards the door and, in a panic, I started running. I stumbled out onto the street and kept on going. Three round, black spheres about the size of footballs came flying towards me. *Ellipsis*, I thought, and threw myself on the ground.

The three balls whizzed over my head, smoke trailing from behind them, then they smashed through the window of the library. There was a moment's silence and then the building exploded into a ball of flame. Glass and brick, books and old table legs flew in all directions. I lay on the floor, my hands covering the back of my head. My ears rang with the noise of the blast. Chunks of debris clattered all over the tarmac around me. When I lifted my head, smoke filled the street and, through it, I could see flames flickering from the ruin of the library.

Tears stung my eyes. I held my breath. Paige Turner and Martin Marvello had been in there when it blew up. My heart thumped in my chest and I stood frozen to the spot, wondering what to do.

Then the smoke cleared and Paige Turner came stumbling out of the smog, carrying Martin Marvello over her shoulder. She had a mobile pressed to her ear. "Hello? Carnegie? Yes, it's Paige. Look it's all gone dog-eared here. Ellipsis missiles. Branch 237 is totalled and the serum is lost. I'm coming in and I'm bringing a civilian..." her eyes locked on me. "Two civilians ..." She started to stride towards me. "Excuse me, young man, I'd like a word with you ..."

Somewhere in the distance, a siren wailed. I'd had enough of **KUNG-FU LIBRARIANS**, spies, FART, Super Reader Serum, **ELLIPSIS MISSILES** and exploding libraries. I turned on my heels and ran. Which is what Paige had told me to do in the first place. I could hear her voice behind me. "We'll catch up with you, young man. We can't leave you wandering free with that serum in your blood. We'll find you, rest assured!"

Chapter 3

3 - 799

MORE SHOPPING TROLLEYS AND OLD BOOTS THAN ACTUAL FISH

I should have run straight home but I was so confused, I didn't know where I was going. Paige Turner's words rang in my ears. They were after me because of this stupid potion stuff. As I ran, I read every sign I passed, every advertisement, no matter how small or big. All the signs in the post office window:

For sale: Duffle coat, floppy hat and red wellingtons, no longer needed.

For sale: Bear skin rug, hardly used. Like new.

Lost: Black and white cat, answers to the name of Tibby.

Found: Talking cat. Won't tell me where it lives.

I read them, every single one without even having to stop and look at them. The words just flew into my head. I'd never even read advertisements like that before. A newspaper blew past and I read it as it flashed by. *And I understood it, instantly!*

"Problems with the Eurozone, America's special relationship with the United Kingdom, Why the Pound is stronger than the Yen, how to get a beach body in thirty days . . ."

My head spun and I stopped and leant against a shop window. What was going on?

The sound of a powerful engine made me turn and I saw a box van. Something about the van made me dive into an alleyway at the side of the shop I was leaning on. I pressed myself against the damp wall and watched as a mobile library drove by. Paige Turner was at the wheel, peering through her pointy glasses, scanning the streets looking for me. Then she was gone. I heaved a sigh of relief and stepped out of the shadows. Everything else seemed normal as I went. People hurried around the shops, hunched against the cold, not looking up. But things weren't normal. I had super reading powers and the SLS were hunting me. How would I ever get home safely? The only person I could think of to go to was Dad and I knew exactly where to find him.

Dad spent most of his time fishing. He loved fishing and so

did I. Or, to be more precise, I loved sitting at the side of the canal next to Dad while we dangled some bread paste stuck to a metal hook into the murky, brown water. I never caught a fish and secretly, I was quite glad about that. Dad didn't have a huge strike rate, either. He caught more shopping trolleys and old boots than actual fish. But I loved the smell of the rusty canal, the quack of the ducks, and the rattle of the rain on the hood of my jacket. Most of all, though, I just loved being with Dad. He never really said much. He never really *did* much either. Apart from fishing.

As expected, Dad sat at the side of the canal as usual. Sometimes, I wonder whether or not he actually went home at all. He just sat there, as still as a mountain, covered in his green waterproofs from his boots up to the pointed peak of his hood. Like a giant garden gnome with his fishing rod stretching out over the canal. I took a breath and tried to calm myself.

"Dad!" I said, hurrying down the steps to the canal side. "Dad!"

"Hi, son," Dad said and fist-bumped me.

"Dad! The library was blown up and there was Martin Marvello, the famous, local, best-selling, award-winning children's author and he had a fight with this librarian and they dropped something on me and it's made me a Super Reader and now they're after me and I don't know what to do!" I said, jumping up and down.

"Wow," Dad replied, waggling his bushy eyebrows. "Busy morning!"

"Honestly, Dad!"

"Here, sit down," Dad said, patting the tackle box that doubled up as a fishing stool next to him. "Take a breath."

I breathed in and stared into the murky waters of the canal. It ran right through the middle of Hinderton, my home town. The buildings were all a rusty brick-red just like the canal. A lot of them were boarded up and there weren't many shops other than charity and pound shops. Lots of people say Hinderton's a dump but I don't think so, I live in a nice warm house and I've got lots of friends.

"I went to the library and got some potion spilt on my head," I explained, slowly. "The librarian there, Paige Turner she's like a secret agent..."

Dad's eyebrows shot up and he stroked his thick beard. "Wish I had your imagination." He smiled.

"But it's true!" I snapped and then looked over to the other people sat along the canal side. There was Billy No-Maggots (Dad called him that because he was always borrowing bait and never had his own), Charlie Chuffin (he always said the word 'chuffin' before anything else, "have you caught any chuffin fish?" that kind of thing) and there was Wheezer, an old man who didn't really say much at all but his breathing was so heavy, he sounded like a steam train. They raised their heads from the water and frowned at me. "Sorry," I said, giving a little wave.

I don't think they heard what I'd said. They all sat near enough to be able to nod and catch your eye but far enough away to be on their own.

"I'm not making it up," I said, sitting back down.

Dad looked troubled and gave his rod a twitch, checking it was secure on the rest. "Maybe you should talk to your mum about this or Anthony . . ."

"What would he know about anything?" I snapped, pulling my knees up to my chin. "He'd think it was great having super reading powers."

"It sounds good . . ." Dad said, looking confused by the whole conversation.

"Well, what superpower would you have if you could have any?" I challenged him.

Dad shrugged. "Dunno," he said.

"Honestly, Dad, of all the superpowers to get, this has to be the worst! Imagine there's an emergency, someone needs rescuing from a burning building. Nobody's going to say, 'If only we had someone who could read really, really quickly!' Or imagine if aliens attacked Earth, they aren't going to run away in fear when they see my awesome reading skills!"

"Right," Dad said, staring across the water. Totally out of his depth.

"Go on, then Dad, how about you? What superpower would you have?"

Dad shrugged and thought for a long time and a brief flicker of sadness crossed his face. "I'd be invisible," he said, at last.

"Invisible? Why?"

He shrugged again then his smile came back as he thought of something. "Better for fishing," he said and nodded at the water rippling as a brown duck sailed past with her ducklings.

I sighed. "I don't know what to do. I'm in big trouble, Dad."

"Have a word with your mum," Dad said. "She usually knows what to do." He stood up and started reeling in his line. I pulled out my phone and my heart plummeted; eighteen missed calls from Mum and twelve from Anthony? I was going to get into mega-trouble now! They probably thought I'd been blown up in the library.

"Dad," I said. "I've got to go. Mum's wondering where I am." She wasn't going to be happy. **I WAS DOOMED!**

Chapter 4

796.8

THE DISBELIEF OF PRISSY MCBEEF

I hurried home, avoiding the whole area around the library and keeping to the alleyways and snickets between houses. I could hear SIRENS, though and a couple of fire engines roared past. POLICE CARS cruised along the streets and people peered from behind their curtains to see what all the fuss was. I didn't see any sign of Paige Turner in her mobile library. As I scurried from street to street, I texted my mates, Prissy and Asif.

Meet me at my place, as soon as you can. Something weird going on.

A moment later two messages flashed back. Asif said:
Ok Matey

Prissy said:

No

This was **TYPICAL** of Prissy McBeef, the most oppositional girl in the world. If you said day, she'd say night. Sometimes, she couldn't help herself. I knew how to help her, though. I texted back:

Don't then, see if I care, up to you

Prissy replied:

OK see you in a few minutes

When I got in, Mum and Anthony were stood, pale-faced on the doorstep. Mum ran and hugged me tight. "Kian, where have you been? We've been worried sick . . ."

Anthony stood at her shoulder, trying to look stern. "When we heard about the gas explosion at the library, we didn't know what to think. We tried phoning you but you didn't answer."

I pulled away from Mum. "I'm fine. I was with Dad. I-I put my phone on silent when we're fishing, don't I?"

"Kian, we were beside ourselves!" Mum said.

I felt my cheeks redden. "Sorry," I muttered. I couldn't tell them about Paige Turner, the SLS and my superpowers could I? They'd think I'd lost it. Anyway, someone had already spread the news that it was a gas leak that caused the explosion. Great.

"I went to get the book but then forgot I said I'd see Dad today, so I went there." My stomach lurched a little more. The book. I hadn't got it. Surely the library blowing up was a good excuse. Somehow, with Mr Vestibule, I didn't think it would be.

Maybe Asif and Prissy would believe me. I've known Asif since Reception and Prissy decided she would be our friend when we started at St Jeffery of the Immaculate Hot Cross Bun Middle School. Asif got a really bad blood infection when he was a baby. That's why he has no thumbs and only two fingers on his left hand and three on the right. Asif got his nickname because all his clothes were fastened with Velcro rather than buttons. The trouble with the name is that some people say it kindly and others use it to upset him. Sometimes, it isn't so much what you say but the way you say it.

Asif and Prissy didn't look at all convinced when I told them about my adventures in the library. Prissy sat at my computer desk, frowning and curling her fingers through her blonde ponytail. Asif raised one eyebrow (one of his party tricks) and pouted his lip.

"So Martin Marvello the famous, local, best-selling, award-winning children's author tried to shoot the librarian?" Asif said, peering closely at me as if I was mad.

"But the librarian duffed him up with Kung Fu," Prissy continued, speaking slowly as if she was talking to a three-year-old. "Because she was a secret agent librarian . . ."

"And now you've got superpowers," Asif finished. They paused for a second, looked at each other and then . . .

"BWAAHAHAHAHAHAHAHAHA!"

They both laughed until I thought they'd **WET** themselves. **HILARIOUS.**

I scowled at them. I should've known they wouldn't believe me. "All right laugh all you want but watch this," I said, handing Asif a telephone directory I'd brought along to demonstrate my new powers. "Ask me any number in that book, any address."

"Okay," Asif said, fumbling through the pages. "Finny, Furry Friends Pet Shop," he said, slamming the directory shut. He looked down. "Oh, I shouldn't have done that. I'll have to find it again.

"It's on page 54," I said, with a smug smile. "But don't bother, I can tell you the number. It's 016753489062. 29, Foreman Street, Hinderton, HL42 6GB."

Asif wrestled around with the pages again and looked at the directory with **WIDE EYES**. "Wow! That's clever!"

"Hmmph!" Prissy snatched the directory from Asif. "Give it here. Okay," she said, frowning and flicking through the pages. "Let's see. Ha! Here we are. J.Smith." She looked hard at me. Deep into my soul. **WILLING ME TO FAIL.** But I didn't!

"Depends *which* J. Smith you're looking at," I said.

"There are eight in the book. They're all on page 405, James Smith 0167 435674, lives at 21 Granby Gardens, another James Smith, 0167234098, lives at Percival Terrace, then Jane Smith 0167524371, lives in Quarmby Street . . ."

Prissy stared, **AMAZED**. She flicked through again. "Okay, where is Crankit Car Repairs?" she said.

"96, West Wallaby Way," I said grinning.

"Rapunzel Hair Design?"

"5, Harbottle Road."

"Pendulum Clocks."

"76 Sands Crescent."

"Kilmartin Rat Repairs?"

I frowned. "Erm . . . I don't remember that one," I said.

"**NO!**"

Prissy said, slamming the directory shut. "I made it up. That's insane, Kian!"

"How did you memorise the directory like that?" Asif said. "It's a neat trick!"

"It's not a trick!" I said, stamping my foot. "I'm telling you. Paige Turner spilt that Reader Serum all over me and it made me a Super Reader!"

Prissy pulled a face. "Reader Serum?" She scoffed. "Is that even a *thing*?"

"It was the only sample of it in the world," I said. "The man who made it was blown up in an explosion and all his notes lost."

"Hmm," Prissy hummed, stroking an imaginary grey beard. "We need a better test."

"He could memorise the works of Shakespeare," Asif suggested. "We could test him . . ."

Prissy glared at Asif. "What do you know about Shakespeare?" she said.

Asif puffed out his chest. "I was Bottom in the school performance of *A Midsummer Night's dream* in year 6, remember?" he said. "I was *born* for Shakespeare . . ."

"Weren't," Prissy said.

"Was," Asif replied.

"You really weren't Asif," I cut in before I went completely mad. "Look, why can't you just believe me?"

"Because librarian spies, an evil organisation called **FART** and super reading powers all sound too far-fetched," Prissy said, she went back to imaginary beard stroking. "No, what we need is some concrete proof. **AHA!**"

"What?" Asif and I said together.

"I have an idea," Prissy said. "I've got a great book that's all about Karate in my bag . . ."

"What's it called?" Asif asked.

"*All About Karate*, funnily enough!" Prissy snapped. "Don't interrupt me again or I'll break your arm."

"I'm not afraid," Asif said. "Did you know, I died twice when I was a baby? Nothing frightens me!"

31

Prissy reached out and Asif yelped, leaping back. "Okay, okay," he said. "No more interruptions!"

"Why have you got a book about karate in your bag?" I asked, frowning.

"It's really thick and **GOOD FOR HITTING PEOPLE WITH**. Never mind that. You read my karate book now," she ordered, "and then on Monday, you can challenge Chadwick to a fight and flatten him using the skills you've learnt from the book!"

"That's mad!" I gasped. Leon Chadwick, the school superstar was brilliant at everything, football, running, lessons and especially gifted at bullying anyone who wasn't brilliant at everything, football, running, lessons and . . . well, you get the idea. He was also a year older than me, as tall as a tower and tough as a tank.

"If you're a Super Reader like you say you are, then you should be able to do it," Prissy said, folding her arms.

"Yeah," Asif said, folding his arms too. "That Chadwick's had it coming for a long time. Always calling me names. I'd deal with him myself but . . ."

"So what do you say, Kian, *Super Reader?*" Prissy said, grinning. "Take on Chadwick and we'll believe you."

"If you win, of course!" Asif added.

"I've got the book here," Prissy said. "You can read it now and then you'll be a black belt before bedtime!"

I felt a stab of anger. "Fine," I said. "You two are meant

to be my friends but if you need absolute proof that I'm not lying then bring it on!"

Prissy grinned and pulled *All About Karate* out of her bag.

At that moment, Anthony popped his head around my bedroom door. "Ooh, sharing books with your friends now?" he said. "Nice one!"

"Leave me alone," I muttered.

"Yeah. Do one Anthony, can't you see we're busy here?" Prissy said. Asif stared in horror and Anthony blinked and then left the room.

I leafed idly through the pages which, because of my new Super Reader powers, meant that I'd finished and absorbed the book in five minutes. "Done it," I said and practised some of the kicks, punches and lunges.

"Wow," Asif said. "Maybe he's telling the truth."

"Of course I am," I said.

"We'll see," Prissy murmured, narrowing her eyes and snatching the book back. "Come on. We've got to go. I've got tap dancing lessons."

I groaned as I shut the door behind them. This wasn't going to work. Chadwick was big and fast. *How can you read yourself into being as athletic as Chadwick? You have to exercise for years, surely*, I thought.

All Sunday, I stayed in my bedroom and practised the moves from the book until I knew I could do every single one.

My tummy still swirled like a **TUMBLE DRYER**. I didn't dare venture out in case Paige Turner was still **SCOURING THE STREETS** in search of me. But, to be honest, I had more pressing worries. That night, my dreams were filled with **CHADWICK'S GRINNING FACE** and **CRUSHING FISTS**. Somehow, though, I didn't think Super Reading Powers were going to be any help at all. And Mr Vestibule would expect me to have the *Improve Your Memory Skills* book.

I WAS DOOMED.

Chapter 4

4 - 796.8

HE'S GOING TO TEAR YOUR WARM, BEATING HEART FROM YOUR CHEST...

Breakfast on any morning is always an awkward business in our house. Anthony, cracks **SAD** jokes about 'cereal killers' and asks if Mum wants more custard on her cornflakes. Even Mum doesn't have much time for Anthony at this time of day. I don't have any, **ANY TIME OF THE DAY!**

This morning, I grabbed my bag and hurried out of the house. I glanced around me, checking for any sign of Paige Turner's mobile library but all I saw were the usual cars and vans going about their business. On top of that, I **STRAINED MY BRAIN** trying to think of a way to **GET OUT** of fighting Chadwick. I dragged my feet on the way to school. I nearly made myself late by walking so slowly but eventually I found myself at the gates, then in the corridor and finally sitting in my seat in class. Of course, I had Mr Vestibule first.

Prissy sat next to me, elbowing Samaira, who normally sat there, out of the way. "Sit in my seat," she said to Samaira, who looked in horror at her.

"But Mr V will go mad at me!" she said. "You know he has a strict seating plan!"

Prissy's eyes widened as if she couldn't believe that Samaira was arguing with her and Samaira decided that it was probably better to be in trouble with Mr Vestibule than with Prissy.

Prissy leant close to me. "So, when are you going to get Chadwick?" she said in a loud voice.

I felt the blood drain from my face. "Will you keep your voice down?" I spluttered. "I was thinking, maybe it's not such a good idea."

"I see," Prissy said, examining her fingernails, theatrically. "So all that about Reader Serum was made up rubbish, was it?"

"No!" I said. "But why do I have to beat up Chadwick to prove it wasn't?"

"It's a controlled test," Prissy said.

"How is it in any way, shape or form controlled?"

"Well," Prissy tried to think of an answer. "I devised it. It's beyond your control, so it's a fair test. You can't influence it unless you use your," she raised two fingers on each hand and drew speech marks in the air, "super powers."

Mr Vestibule swept into the room before I could reply. "McBeef either sit in your proper place or go and sit outside the Head's office, I don't mind which."

Prissy narrowed her eyes and tried to fire laser bolts out of them at Mr Vestibule but nothing happened. I could see her problem. Prissy needed to defy people most of the time, she couldn't help it, her brain was just wired that way. Mr Vestibule had short-circuited any argument by giving her two choices and saying he wasn't bothered which she took.

She's on the **HORNS OF A DILEMMA**, I thought. Then I blinked. *Where did that expression come from?*

Finally, Prissy slunk over to her desk and Samaira sat back in her place next to me.

"This lesson, as part of the school-wide focus on functional literacy, we will be reading some non-fiction texts," Mr. Vestibule said, dragging a large box from under his desk. "Asif, you can give out the books and then we are each going to take a turn reading aloud."

Everyone started to grumble but Mr. Vestibule gave one look and silence fell like a **BLANKET OF QUIETNESS** over them. The only noise was **ASIF GRUNTING** as he struggled with the box and the **THUD** of the huge textbooks as they hit the tables. I was waiting for Mr V to use the time to ask me if I visited the library at the weekend but he seemed preoccupied, scanning the room and looking from child to child.

Once the books were handed out, Mr Vestibule settled himself in his chair and opened his own copy. "Now, let's see, who shall we start with?" he said.

Asif threw his hand in the air, making little squeaking noises to indicate he was very keen to have a go. "*Me! Sir, Me!*"

Not me, not me, I thought. *Not me!*

Mr Vestibule fixed me with his steely gaze and smirked. "Ah, Reader. Off you go."

My heart PLUMMETED as I opened the book and my head spun as my eyes made contact with the words. "The main problem with the economy in 1918 was that the world was still reeling from the devastating effects of the Great War ..."

"Stop!" Mr. Vestibule said. He stared at me, his eyes almost GLOWED WITH EXCITEMENT. I felt my cheeks reddening. "Well, Kian," Mr Vestibule said. "What did you have for breakfast this morning? I've never heard anyone read quite so ... fast ..."

I looked down at the book to avoid Mr Vestibule's gaze but the words leapt up from the page at me, information flooding into my brain. I snapped my eyes up again. "Sorry, sir."

"Not at all, not at all," Mr Vestibule said, still grinning. "It's very good, Kian, very promising in fact. Carry on."

I sighed and read on, desperately trying to slow myself down. Have you ever noticed that when you can do something REALLY EASILY, it's hard to do it slowly or to pretend to be bad at it? You end up feeling all frustrated and bottled up because you've made yourself lose a game or go really slowly. Well, that's what I felt like.

Mr Vestibule sat nodding and scribbling notes in a pad. Finally, he stopped me. "Excellent work, Kian, you have excelled yourself. Jenny Smith, carry on reading."

Jenny Smith reddened and took over from where I left off. I glanced around at Prissy but she **GLARED** at her pen top, as usual. Even Asif looked away when I tried to catch his eye.

The lesson dragged on and when everyone had read, Mr. Vestibule insisted on asking questions. **NOT ME, DON'T ASK ME,** I thought, clenching my fists and screwing my eyes shut. I remembered Dad saying he would have invisibility as a superpower and wished for the same thing.

"Kian," Mr. Vestibule said. "Who was President of America in 1918?"

"Woodrow Wilson, sir," I said, before I could stop myself. "Born December 28, 1856 and died February 3, 1924."

"Interesting!" Mr. Vestibule said. "And what made the recession in Germany deeper than in other parts of Europe?"

"The Treaty of Versailles meant that Germany had to pay money to the other countries," I said, the words just flowing. "This caused a lot of resentment and was one of the things that led to the growth of the Nazi party in later years."

Mr. Vestibule almost **STOOD UP AND CLAPPED**. He nodded.

"Superb, Kian," he said. "I don't know what has come over you but obviously, this is amazing progress."

I felt my face REDDEN LIKE A RIPE TOMATO again and I felt guilty because part of me was pleased with Mr. Vestibule's comments. A little part of me felt smug too. If I was honest, I was showing off. I grinned over at Prissy, who glared at me as if I'd pulled off some kind of magic trick.

"Well done, Kian," Mr. Vestibule said, standing next to Prissy's table. "I wish some *other pupils* would be as attentive as you."

I looked at the floor, ashamed for smiling at the teacher's praise. I could feel Prissy's eyes burning a hole in the back of my blazer.

The class was dismissed and I found Asif in the corridor. "It wasn't me," I said. "It was the Reader Serum!"

"Whatever," Asif said, he gave a weak smile. "Hey, anyway, it's good right? Maybe you'll go up a set."

"But I don't want to be like this," I said. "I . . ."

"Oh, here he is," Prissy McBeef said crashing into me. "MR KNOW-IT-ALL," she put her hands on her hips, waggled her head from side to side and put on a sing-song voice. "Woodvale Watson, sir, The Treaty of Verse Eye, sir . . . Well done, Kian . . . Hurp!" Prissy pretended to spew up.

"It's Woodrow Wilson," I said. "And it's all one word Versaille. I can't help it if I'm . . ." I clammed up, killing the words before they came out.

But Prissy had caught onto what I was going to say. "If you're what?" she said, glaring at me. "Smarter than us? Is that it?"

"No!" I said. "Oh no!" The last part of this statement was directed at Chadwick who had just come out of the boy's toilets.

Prissy gave me a wicked grin and turned round. "Hey Chadwick," she yelled. "My mate, Kian is a **BLACK BELT** at Karate and he's going to **TEAR YOUR WARM BEATING HEART** from your chest, now."

Chadwick strode forwards. "Is that right?" he said. "Well, **I'M A BLACK BELT AT FIST-FU** and this knuckle sandwich is all Kian's."

"Fist-Fu?" Asif interrupted. "What's that?"

Chadwick glared at him. "I made it up. I'll give you a demonstration once I've planted Reader" he said, grinning and smacking his fist into his palm.

"Go on Kian," Prissy said. "Give 'im hell!"

I stood with my legs wide and put out my hands. But I couldn't remember what I'd had read in the Karate book. It had all gone. All the knowledge I'd absorbed on Sunday morning had vanished!

"**HIIIYAAA!**" I yelled, and stamped my foot down, trying to be as convincing as possible. Chadwick grinned and lashed out with his fist.

THWACK!

Fireworks blossomed before my eyes and my head spun.

I staggered backwards and felt the world turn upside down as Chadwick gripped me in a wrestling hold and dumped me headfirst into a *nearby litter bin*. The smell of stale yoghurt filled my nostrils and I felt something slimy on my face.

Chadwick's voice sounded muffled because of the bin. "Looks like you need to practise your Kung Fu a little bit more," he said.

Slowly, the weight of my body pulled the bin to its side and I lay, listening to the laughter that echoed round the busy corridor. I'd never live this down and it was all Prissy McBeef's fault.

AHA! NOTHING TO WORRY ABOUT.

"How is it my fault?" Prissy said, standing with her hands on her hips and a **MASSIVE SCOWL** that brought her bottom lip and her eyebrows in close contact.

"You didn't believe me, like a friend should," I snapped. "You set me up to fight Chadwick ..."

"Well if you'd been telling the truth, then you would have *beaten* Chadwick!" Prissy yelled back. Her face was red and a bit of spit flew out of her mouth. "You just stood there with your hands out. You read the book, didn't you?"

I frowned and scratched my head. "Yeah, I did but I couldn't remember any of it," I said. "It was like it had all vanished."

"Maybe the knowledge only lasts for a short time," Asif said. "I read a story once about a boy who could turn into a wolf

43

but only for five hours . . ."

"Maybe," I said, still glaring at Prissy. "But that's not the point!"

"And what is the point?" Prissy growled, squaring up to me.

"The point is it was your stupid idea to . . ."

Prissy's face went from red to pale white (if that's possible). "Stupid?" she hissed. "Did you say I was *STUPID?*"

"I said your idea was stupid not . . ."

But Prissy wasn't listening, she grabbed Asif by the elbow. "Come on Asif, we're not *CLEVER* enough to hang out with Mr Kian Super Reader anymore," she said and frog-marched Asif away down the corridor.

"But I am clever!" Asif protested. "I was born clever!"

"No you weren't," Prissy said. Asif didn't even to try and argue back.

Most kids had gone into their next lesson now and I stood in the empty corridor feeling so alone. Mr Vestibule appeared outside his classroom. "Ah, Reader," he said. "Just the person I was looking for. Go down to the medical room at once. The school doctor wants to have a look at you."

"At me, sir? What for?"

Mr Vestibule tried to smile, which was awful; he looked like he'd trapped his finger in the door. "Just routine. Everyone's having a check-up. Run along, now."

I shrugged. *Fair enough*, I thought, *it gets me out of Maths.*

The Medical Room was at the front of the school but down a quiet corridor that ran past the office and the staff toilets. I knocked on the green door and it creaked open.

An incredibly TALL AND THIN man stood looking down at me. His long, white coat made him look even taller and thinner. He reminded me of a STICK INSECT, except his coat was white and stick insects are brown and don't wear coats. But he still reminded me of a stick insect . . . a white one . . . in a lab coat. His shiny, bald head was long like a PEANUT and he tilted it to one side. He wore a monocle that was dark like a sunglasses lens. His other watery, blue eye flicked from my head to my toes and back again. He also looked very familiar but I couldn't think why.

"You must be the boy that Vestibule sent to me," he said. His voice sounded smooth, oily and very posh. Sometimes Anthony would put on a posh accent and said "Hurricanes hardly ever happen in Hereford or Hampshire!" It sounded more like "Haracyanes Hardly Hever Harpen in Herefyord or Hampshyar." That's what this man sounded like. "Do come in," the doctor said, throwing the door back.

The medical room looked like it always did. A trolley bed lined one side of the small room and a plastic chair stood beside it. The man pointed at the bed. "Sit there," he said and pulled out what looked like a torch from his pocket.

I sat on the bed and the man shone a torch into my eye. "My name is Doctor Badd," the man said. "That with a B and an A and a double, double D. This is just the routine check-up from the neck up ... *AHA!*"

I nearly **JUMPED OFF THE BED**. "What?" I said, my heart thumping.

Doctor Badd pulled a face. "Nothing," he said and wrapped a tape-measure round my head. "*AHA!*"

Again, I nearly jumped through the ceiling. "What?" I said, trembling. "What?"

Doctor Badd shrugged. "Average," he said. "Hold still." He pulled a box from his pocket and screwed what looked like a stethoscope tube into it. Then he looked at a sheet of paper and frowned. "You have an unusual name."

"Y-yes, sir," I said, wincing a little as the cold metal at the end of the stethoscope tube pressed against my forehead.

"And are you?" Doctor Badd asked.

I felt my cheeks redden and I pretended that the stupid joke wasn't about to come. "Erm, am I what, sir?"

A broad smile cracked Doctor Badd's pale face, making the skin on his bald head wrinkle. "**A KEEN READER**. Eh? Geddit? Kian ... keen ..."

I stifled the groan of despair that boiled in my stomach. "No," I said quietly. "Not really."

"What?" Doctor Badd said, frowning. "You don't get the joke or you don't like reading?"

"I don't like reading, sir," I said. "And actually, it's pronounced

Kee- an." In fact, what I felt like screaming was, "NO! I HATE BOOKS! THEY'RE STUPID AND BORING AND I'D RATHER STICK KNITTING NEEDLES IN MY EYES THAN READ A RUBBISH BOOK!"

"Excellent!" Doctor Badd said, but I wasn't sure if that meant it was good that I didn't like books or that my name was pronounced 'Kee-an.' A little light bleeped on the box that Doctor Badd was holding. "AHA!" he said.

I looked at him expectantly but Doctor Badd shook his head. "Nothing much," he said. He looked up at me and gave the briefest of smiles. At least I think it was a smile. He kind of showed me his teeth. "Thank you, perfect . . . I mean nothing to worry about, just wait here and I'll be back in a moment."

Doctor Badd left the room and I heard the lock click. It was then that I realised where I had seen him before. He was the tall, thin man who stood behind the mayor with Mr Vestibule! The mayor who had been hypnotised like Martin Marvello! Doctor Badd was a member of FART and possibly Mr Vestibule too! They must have been searching for me because I had the serum splashed on my head! I had to get out quickly. But how?

Chapter 6

6 - 649

THAt wAs A SimilE, you BuFFoon!

Looking around the Medical Room, I realised that there was **NO WAY OUT**. There were no windows and only one door which was locked. I hurried to the door to test it as if I hadn't heard Doctor Badd turn the key. Then footsteps clicked down the corridor outside.

"He's the boy," Doctor Badd's voice echoed through the door. "The brain scan showed he'd been exposed to the Super Reader Serum. We can use him as a pawn in our complicated chess game with the SLS."

"Why are we playing chess with the SLS, Doctor?" another voice said. "I thought this was all about world domination and the destruction of books!"

Badd sighed. "It was a metaphor, right? I was making our

plan seem complicated and clever . . ."

"Ah. I see," the voice replied. "Amazing."

The key turned in the lock and I **PRESSED MYSELF AGAINST THE WALL** at the side of the door as the doctor stepped into the room. He was flanked by two bald-headed men, dressed in black uniforms and wearing sunglasses, even though it was a dull October day.

"Where is he?" one man muttered, not noticing that I was behind them.

In the split second that the door stood unguarded, I slid out and began running down the corridor. "Oi!" the man shouted after me.

"Don't just stand there like a **CONFUSED WATER BUFFALO**, you fools, get after him!"

"A confused water buffalo, doctor? What do you mean?"

"That was a simile, you buffoon! Did you never do English in school?" Badd snapped.

"Well, not really . . ."

"GET AFTER HIM!" Badd bellowed.

The two men's boots clattered on the polished tiles but I'd already slammed past the office and out of the front door. As luck would have it, a parent was just coming in and I didn't have to worry about the automatic locking. I vaulted over the old metal school gate and sprinted down the street, not daring to look back once. I assumed the two men would still be after me, but I couldn't hear their footsteps anymore.

Once again, advertisements on the sides of buses, on huge billboards and in shop windows flashed by and I soaked them up, trying not to read them. Cars whizzed past, lorries and vans, their engine noise becoming deafening. Where could I go? Dad. Surely, he'd know what to do. I hurried to the steps at the side of the road and down to the canal.

It felt calmer down by the water. The high stone walls of the cutting that had been dug out centuries ago to keep the canal level seemed to soak up the noise of the town. Dad sat in his usual place, wrapped in his green waterproofs, rod leaning out across the water. He raised his bushy eyebrows when I sat down next to him.

"School?" he said.

I lowered my head between my knees and got my breath back. "I ran out of school," I said.

"Why's that?" Dad said, still staring at the float.

"I had a fight," I said. "And lost and then this weird doctor measured my head and two goons tried to kidnap me."

Dad's brow furrowed in confusion. "What for?"

"Because of my super reading powers, of course."

"Oh," he said, with a brief nod. "That one again."

I felt a sting of anger. "What d'you mean?" I snapped. "You've got to believe me!"

Dad turned and looked at me. "Look son, you've got to stop

this . . . this . . . thing you have about books and reading," he said. "I mean it's okay to have a good imagination but running out of school just to get out of reading . . ."

"There's nothing wrong with my reading. Apart from I can read EVERYTHING all at once. Anyway, I hate reading, I hate books, I hate libraries and I hate bloomin' Anthony always going on about how great reading is and how it changed his life and . . ."

"It's true," Dad said.

I stared at Dad. "What?"

"It's true," Dad said again. "Reading *is* great. I wish I'd read more when I was a kid. Maybe I'd be better at reading now. Maybe I'd have been smarter at school and got a decent job. And that Anthony's all right. He makes your mum happy which is more than I ever did."

I flapped my mouth up and down, probably looking like one of the fish Dad hardly ever caught. I'd never heard Dad say more than three or four words strung together and I never expected him to defend Anthony. "You . . . but I thought you were on my side . . ."

"There are no sides, Kian. If you've got a talent, Kian, you should be using it," Dad said, fixing me with his steely blue eyes. "Not making up stories and running out of school."

I could feel tears scalding my eyes now. "I'm not making it up! Why won't you believe me? Why is everyone against me?"

"I'm not against you, Kian. Nobody is. You've just got to accept that and get on with your life."

"What like you have?" I snapped, feeling sick as I said the words.

Dad's face hardened. "What's that meant to mean?"

"You just sit here all day every day. You don't even catch anything. You don't even try. You're meant to help me but instead, you're just staring at a little orange float in the water. I hate you!"

I jumped to my feet, my stomach churned as I turned and ran up the towpath towards home. The worst part was the way Dad had just stared at me as I snapped at him. He didn't look angry, just sad and helpless.

I came to the house and stopped. The front door hung open. The house looked empty and as I approached it, it felt quiet and deserted, not like a home that someone has just left but like something was missing. Mum was working at the Cheapsave Supermarket like she always did but Anthony was always at home on a Monday. He always got time off in lieu which meant that he took Monday off from the office because he worked Saturdays. "I've got time off in the loo," he always said. But I didn't need my bad joke censor to tell me he wasn't in the house, I just knew.

The door creaked as I stepped into the hall, it sounded loud and seemed to echo all over the house, announcing my presence. A crackling sound came from the television in the front living room and I could see the screen flickering. Books lay strewn around, pages ripped and covers torn. And Anthony was nowhere to be seen.

YOU ARE PROBABLY WONDERING

I stepped into the room. My laptop was connected to the television. Puzzled, I leant down and tapped a key. A white coat filled the television screen and a long chin just poked down from the top of the picture.

"Hello, Kian Reader." I caught my breath. My scalp prickled. It was **DOCTOR BADD!** "You are probably wondering . . ." He stopped, obviously realising that his head was out of shot. He bent double, bringing his face close to the screen. "Blast this stupid technology. There!" He stepped back and I could see his long head, like an **EVIL PEANUT** and his dark monocle glinting in the dull light. He was standing in our living room, so I guessed this was a recording and not a live video link or something.

"So, where was I? Ah! Yes, hello, Kian Reader. You are

probably wondering . . ." **AN ICE CREAM VAN** drove by outside, its chimes drowning Doctor Badd's voice. Doctor Badd cursed under his breath and turned to someone out of shot. "Shut that stupid noise up at *once!*" He turned back to the screen. "You are probably wondering . . ." the camera suddenly slid, and all I could see was Doctor Badd's coat pocket. Obviously the laptop had fallen off something and landed on its side. I could hear Badd grumbling and hissing curses under his breath. "Ridiculous thing! I should have brought my own . . ."

"Best not to balance it on the arm of the sofa, boss," said a deep voice off screen.

"I know! I know!" Doctor Badd yelled, shaking a gloved fist at someone I couldn't see. I watched as the room swirled before him on the screen and suddenly the laptop was resting on something stable, I worked out that it was the chest of draws that stood at the side of the room. "There!" said Doctor Badd. "You are probably wondering what has happened to your beloved family member, Anthony, *BEHOLD!*" Doctor Badd stepped aside to reveal the television.

"Uh, you moved the laptop, boss, he's over here," said the voice off-camera again.

"You think I don't know that?" Doctor Badd muttered. "Don't be so insolent. You think I don't know? You think you've got what it takes to be a criminal mastermind? Eh? No, I didn't think so!" He twisted the laptop and I gasped. "Right, how's that?"

The image on the screen panned across the room. Anthony sat on our sofa, ropes binding his arms and what looked like the pages of a book STUFFED IN HIS MOUTH to gag him. Two identical, burly guards dressed in black combat gear and wearing sunglasses stood either side of him, looking evil and menacing. Any other time, I would have paid good money to see that happen to Anthony but now I just felt sick.

"You might have escaped from us this morning but we found your address. This character got in our way. So," Doctor Badd said. "This is what is going to happen. You will go to Hinderton Central Library and give yourself up to Paige Turner. She will take you to SLS HQ. Once you are inside, you will find the instruction manual for SLS HQ and you will read it. Once you have done that, you will leave the SLS headquarters and you will meet me in the school playground at midnight tonight with all that lovely information in your head. Tell nobody about what you are doing. If you do it will be THE CURTAINS for Anthony . . ."

One of the guards gave an embarrassed cough. "Will he know what that means, boss?" he said. "I mean, the whole 'curtains' thing . . . he's only a kid . . ."

"Do you have to interrupt everything I say?" Doctor Badd snapped. "He knows what 'the curtains' means . . ."

"Sorry boss, I erm . . . it's JUST 'curtains' boss, not 'the curtains,'" the guards mumbled, scratching his head. "It's curtains for Anthony, not 'THE curtains'."

Doctor Badd's face filled the screen. "I think he knows what will happen if he does not comply with my wishes," he said, quietly. "Now read this." Badd held up a sheet of written instructions and I couldn't help but absorb every detail of what I had to do. I noticed a few spelling mistakes and one of the sentences didn't quite make sense either, but I got the gist.

"Remember, you tell nobody, understand?" Doctor Badd said. The screen went dark as Doctor Badd leant into it. "Well, that went better than I thought it would," he said. "Is it off? How do you stop it recording? Let me do it, how do you think I will learn if you keep doing things for me? Oh . . ." The sound screen went dead.

I sat staring at the laptop. Anthony, Mum's New Boyfriend, had been kidnapped and only I could save him! I stood amongst the flapping, torn up pages of Anthony's books, my mind whirling. *Mum's going to be worried sick*, I thought.

"I've got to get Anthony back," I said aloud.

I looked around. *She'll blame me for this mess! Maybe she'll think I had something to do with Anthony's disappearance. She'd be right. I do! If I hadn't run away from Paige Turner, maybe none of this would have happened.*

One thing was certain, if Mum came home and saw the mess and found Anthony missing, she'd phone the police and that would make matters even more complicated. I needed to buy some time. I grabbed the laptop and typed up a letter:

Dear Chris, (That's Mum's name)

I've been called away on business. I'll be away in Brighton for a few days buying supplies and stuff. I'll be back on Friday. I'll give you a call when I get to my hotel.

Yours sincerely,

Anthony.

That should do it, I thought. *Good job we did letter writing in class last week. If I'd put 'Yours faithfully' when Anthony knows Mum's name, she would've rumbled it straight away!* I looked around at the mess. It looked like a gorilla who really hates books had been let loose in the house. Paper fluttered everywhere, book covers lay strewn across the floor.

P.S. (I wrote at the bottom of the letter)

I'm having a clear out of books so don't worry about the mess.

I gave a grunt of satisfaction as I read the note again, then thought I'd better leave one of my own, just in case I was late back.

Gone night fishing with Dad.

Love Kian x

I hope that doesn't get Dad into trouble, I thought. As quickly as I could, I scrambled around, snatching up loose pages and torn books and threw as many of them as I could into the recycling bin. Words flashed through my head, whole paragraphs SLITHERED INTO MY MIND. Facts, fragments of information all jumbled together in my brain like a big word soup. And all the time, questions kept BOBBING TO THE SURFACE OF THE SOUP. Why did Doctor Badd want him to read the SLS Headquarters Manual? How come I couldn't remember the karate moves I'd read about on Sunday? I tried to remember the numbers from the telephone directory that Prissy and Asif had tested me with but it was a blank. Maybe Asif was right, maybe the Super Reader Serum only let me remember something for a short while, say, twenty four hours or something.

I shrugged off the questions, maybe I could find out later but right now, I needed to rescue Anthony and that meant finding Paige Turner and the SLS.

THE FLYING MOBILE LIBRARY

It was getting late as I walked along the streets towards the Hinderton Central Library. A huge, old, red-brick building, it stood in the centre of town. People hurried home from work, weaving between each other on the darkening pavement. Cars were putting their headlights on and the shop windows glowed. Mum would be back home soon to discover the house empty. I felt a stab of guilt. *I wonder if school will tell her that I ran home this afternoon*, I thought. *Mum will be even more worried, then.*

As I walked, I couldn't help feeling that I was **BEING WATCHED**, maybe even **FOLLOWED**. I glanced behind every now and then but only saw tired commuters carrying briefcases, late shoppers lugging bags around or pushing prams.

The feeling didn't go away. I glimpsed a dark figure ducking behind a car. A **FLASH** of a black coat as someone slipped into a shop doorway to avoid being seen. Who could it be? I wondered, Men from FART checking up on me? I thought back to the two burly henchmen with dark glasses on and shuddered.

CRASH!

I spun around, convinced someone was about to pounce on me. Asif lay sprawled across a pile of potatoes that were on a display counter outside the greengrocer shop. Potatoes and onions rolled around the pavement, **A COUPLE OF CARROTS JOINED IN TOO**, and Prissy McBeef stood glaring at Asif.

"You *IDIOT!*" Prissy yelled. "I said we had to be stealthy!"

"I *was* being stealthy," Asif said, picking himself up and plonking a few rogue turnips back on the grocery stall. "I was *born* stealthy!"

I groaned. "What do you want?" I said.

"We've been following you," Prissy said.

"I know," I replied. "What for?"

"We were worried about you —" Asif began.

"*HE* was worried about you," Prissy cut in. "When he disappeared today, he kept going on about you not being safe on your own and acting strange."

"Acting strange?" I said.

"Well, all the Super Reader stuff . . ." Asif said, looking apologetic. "It's a bit far-fetched, matey but then when you pulled that stunt in the classroom with the reading around the class, I was **GOB-SMACKED**."

"So what's going on?" Prissy said. "We came around to your house and it was all dark. We saw you sneaking off. Where are you going?"

"And can we help?" Asif added.

"No," I said. I couldn't tell them anything more. If Doctor Badd found out and they messed things up, it would be curtains for Anthony. And I had a pretty good idea what that meant. "I'm not doing anything. I'm just going to the library . . ."

"But you *HATE* the library!" Prissy said. "Why would you want to go there?"

I avoided Prissy's piercing gaze. It could melt lies like **SUPERMAN'S HEAT VISION**. "Not anymore," I said. "Now I've got my Super Reader powers, I want to try them out even more!" I had a flash of inspiration. "I'm testing my limits!" I said. "I couldn't remember anything from that karate book and I think there's a time-limit on the information I absorb."

"*Great!* We can help," Asif said. "You see I thought that too. I thought that maybe the information lasts for twenty-four hours. You read Prissy's book on Saturday evening but by Monday morning, it had gone. Let's go . . ."

"No," I said. "I have to do this on my own."

"But why?" Prissy insisted.

My stomach **KNOTTED UP** like one of Dad's fishing lines with an eel wriggling around it. The clock was ticking and I couldn't tell them anything. "I just do! Okay? There's nothing to help with. Just leave me alone and stop following me!"

Asif's face dropped and he looked at me with his huge, brown eyes. Prissy folded her arms. She looked angry but I could tell she was hurt too. "Go on then," she said. "Go to your *stupid* library, see if we care. Libraries are stupid anyway. You said so yourself. And so is reading. Come on Asif!"

"I quite like libraries," Asif said, running after Prissy. "And reading. I was *born* reading . . ."

I sighed and watched them go. For a second, I wanted to **CALL THEM BACK** and tell them everything but I couldn't. I turned and started towards the library at running pace. I had to get there right away.

The Central Library was much bigger and busier than the little branch I'd visited on Saturday. There were grown-ups working on the computers and some older kids I half recognised from school making notes at the tables by the bookshelves. A harassed-looking dad was leafing through picture books while his little girl threw herself across the beanbags and cushions in the comfy corner. I read every title of every book on every bookshelf I passed. Instantly.

Paige Turner's eyebrows shot up as I approached the check-out desk. "You," she hissed, glancing around to make sure nobody was listening. "We've been looking high and low for you."

"I want to know more about this serum stuff," I said, glancing around. "The last few days have been mad. I can't stop *reading* things!" I decided not to mention Doctor Badd, as that might make Paige Turner suspicious.

She sniffed. "Well, if you'd come back to headquarters with me in the first place, you'd have saved yourself a lot of *unpleasantness*, I'm sure," she said, looking at her watch. "You can't walk around with that kind of power. What if FART were to find out?" She turned to a young woman who was tapping something into a computer at the other end of the counter. "Carrel," Paige said. "I'm going to have to leave you in charge. *The boy* has turned up again!"

Carrel turned around and smiled at me. "So you're *the boy*," she said. "I've heard a lot about you. I'm Carrel Filler, librarian and," she glanced around to make sure nobody was listening, "SLS, 004."

My eyes widened. "004, is that your spy number? Like *James Bond*?"

Carrel nodded. "It is but I don't have one of those licence to kill thingies," she said. "Every spy has a number based on the Dewey Decimal System used for ordering books. My job's computing and IT. 004."

"Oh," I said, trying not to sound too disappointed.

"So, do you have a name or are we just going to call you *the boy* for the rest of your life?"

I shook her hand. "Erm, I'm Kian," he said. "Kian Reader..."

Her eyes lit up. "Really?" she said, smiling warmly. "We'll have to compare notes; everyone seems to have an unusual name around here! D'you get lame jokes all the time? Have to repeat your name and convince people that it really *is* your name? That sort of thing?"

"Yeah," I grinned in spite of everything. I liked Carrel.

Paige bustled out of the back office. "Come along, no time for shilly-shallying," she said. "Will you be all right, Carrel?"

"There's half an hour until we close," she said. "What can possibly go wrong?"

"Well, there was that invasion of Brownies last month," Paige said. "They were on some kind of treasure hunt-type game, looking for a particular book. Took us ages to shoo them out!"

Carrel smiled. "My ninja training came in handy that night, I can tell you," she said.

I stared at her, trying to see if she was joking or not but Carrel just turned back to her screen and carried on working.

"This way," Paige said and hurried towards the exit.

The mobile library that I had seen Paige driving on Friday night stood in the car park, waiting for them. Paige pointed her key fob at it and unlocked the door. I climbed up into the passenger seat and slammed the door shut.

"Right, now," Paige muttered, FLICKING A FEW SWITCHES. The dashboard gave a bleep and the front slid away to reveal a complicated panel of flashing lights and switches. "Shadow mode engaged," she said, pressing a button. "In stealth mode. Good. We're invisible to infrared, ultraviolet, radar and eyesight. Are you strapped in? Good."

Paige slammed her foot down on the accelerator and there was a ROAR OF ROCKETS behind them. My stomach plummeted down, took a right and a left at my underpants, shot past my knees and thudded into my socks as the mobile library lifted off the ground.

"WOOOHOOOO!" Paige yelled, skimming over the red-tiled rooftops. "Hold onto your hat, kidder, Sky Library, here we come!" Which is not what you expect an elderly librarian to shout . . . ever.

NINJA LIBRARIANS OF OXFORD

Hinderton shrank beneath us. The cars looked like toys and the canal grew thinner and thinner until the whole town became a SMUDGE OF RED AND BROWN amongst a patchwork quilt of green fields. I noticed a stubby wing sticking out of the side of the van. *We're flying*, I thought, gripping the door handle with white knuckles. *In a mobile library.*

"Ooh, feeling a bit QUEASY are we darling?" Paige Turner said, rummaging in her pocket. She pulled out a boiled sweet. "Here. Have this."

"What flavour is it?" I said. "I don't like lime . . ."

"It's not a sweetie, it's an ANTI-NAUSEA PILL," she said. "It'll stop you throwing up all over the dashboard. Imagine the shame of plummeting to our deaths because of a little bit of vomit . . ."

I took the pill and looked down again. White fluffy clouds masked the land now. "So, the Sky Library is . . ."

"Headquarters for the SLS," Paige said. "It's where everything happens!"

"I thought quite a lot had been happening down there," I muttered.

"I mean, it's where we get our missions, people are trained. And it's where we meet our boss, Carnegie."

Before I could ask any more questions, the clouds parted to reveal a **HUGE FLYING, FLAT DISC**. The top of the disc was a landing strip with numerous mobile libraries parked on it. A tall control tower poked out of the middle of the space. The sides of the disc had windows dotted all around it and a column poked down towards the earth, bristling with aerials and satellite dishes.

"Someone likes their television programs," I said.

"**INFORMATION**," Paige replied. "That's what libraries are all about. Whether it's on paper or electronic, it's all information. Do you think I just spend my day putting books in alphabetical order?"

"Well . . ."

"Shut up, we're landing," Paige snapped. The landing strip grew bigger as the mobile library drew closer and, even though it looked huge, I started to worry whether we would actually land without flying off the other end. "Always a bit tricky, this landing business," Paige muttered. "Normally get Carrel to do it. I'm rubbish at reverse parking too."

The blood drained from my face as the surface of the Sky Library drew *closer* and **CLOSER**. Then, with a **BUMP** we landed and Paige slammed the brakes on.

"Phew," she said, blowing a loose strand of grey hair out of her face. "Made it!" She drove the van alongside several others and climbed out.

A chill wind cut through my thin jacket when I opened the door. Paige strode across the landing platform towards the tower in the middle. I could see windows in it now and a door at the bottom. Paige pulled open the door and led me into an elevator. Her finger hovered over the number pad at the side.

"This is always a bit of a worrying moment too," she said and smiled at me briefly.

"Why?"

"Well, if I get the code wrong, lasers fire from the walls at three levels and eight angles," she grinned. "We'll be **CUT UP LIKE A BIRTHDAY CAKE**. I'm terrible with numbers and passwords and the like."

"Really?" I said, staring around the cramped elevator in horror.

"I'm sure it'll be fine," Paige smiled.

I watched **INTENTLY** as she punched the numbers. *If I need to get out of here fast, I don't want to be stuck or sliced up*, I thought.

335.216.

The lift jerked into life and once again, my stomach lurched. We stood waiting as the lift whirred us downwards.

Finally, the door slid open and I gazed out onto a brightly lit room, lined with bookshelves. Rows of computers sat beneath a huge screen that filled the wall on one side of the room.

A smartly-dressed woman met us at the lift. "Paige," said the woman, smiling. "So, this is the boy?"

"Yes," Paige said. "Kian, this is Kazu Tanaka Agent 796.8, Head of Strategic Physical Interventions . . ."

"Oh," I said, not understanding a word.

Kazu laughed and her eyes widened. "I run the Ninja Librarians of Oxford," she said. "Don't ever let a book go overdue down there!"

I followed as Kazu led them across the room. "Be careful of that . . ." She began to say, pointing at a bookcase. Suddenly the ground shifted beneath me and **CRUNCH** I fell on my bottom. I tried to stand up and fell over again. Eventually, I managed to crawl past the bookcase. "What was that?" I panted.

Kazu and Paige laughed. "You have to be careful, there," Kazu said. "It's the Non-Friction section!"

"Really?" I looked at the small bookcase.

"Books can be dangerous, Kian," Paige said. "The Sky Library has the most dangerous collection of books known! There's something about the information in those books that affects reality around them, making the floor slippy. We don't really understand them."

"But if they're dangerous," I said, "why don't you just get rid of them?"

"Because in different hands it might be used as a force for good," she said, smiling at me.

"Even if they're dangerous?" I said.

"All books can be dangerous, Kian," Paige said, waving her arms at the library around her. "Think of a road atlas in the hands of an invading army, a book on human anatomy read by a serial killer. Any book can be dangerous."

"So books are bad then?" I said. "I knew it!"

"The books aren't bad. It's who uses them and what for. Think of a road atlas in the hands of an ambulance driver, a book on human anatomy in the hands of a child who dreams of being a doctor," Paige's eyes grew dreamy and distant. "What d'you get then?"

"A botched attempt at an operation on the kid next door?" I said.

"TRUST YOU!" Paige said and turned to Kazu. "Have you seen Professor Petri? He'll be eager to see Kian."

Before Kazu could reply, a voice cried out behind them. "Is this the boy?"

I turned to see a small man with a shock of white hair and thick, bottle-end spectacles squinting at me.

"This is Kian Reader," Paige said. "The boy who was soaked with the Reader Serum, professor."

Professor Petri **POKED ME WITH A BALLPOINT PEN**. "*Excellent,*" he said. "And it works I believe?"

"Er, yes," I said, with a shrug.

"Any headaches? Dizziness?"

I shook my head. "No."

"VOMITING?"

"No," I said, starting to feel worried.

"DIARRHOEA? EXCESSIVE WIND?"

"No. Should there be?" I said.

"No, no, no," Professor Petri said, he peered at me again. "How about nightmares or hallucinations?"

"No, I feel fine," I said, not feeling fine at all.

"Murderous thoughts?"

"Petri! You're **WORRYING** the boy," Paige said. "He was in perfect health when he ran away from me."

"That's good, that's good!" Petri said, nodding. "Come with me and we'll check you over."

Professor Petri led me out of the library room and along a corridor. Everything was white: white floor, white walls, white strip lights. It reminded me of a hospital more than a library. We stepped into a room that was full of beds and medical equipment.

"Just lie on the bed," Petri said. I climbed onto the hospital bed and Petri began to strap monitors on my forehead. "Roll your sleeves up," Petri said and more monitors were applied to my arms.

The tests seemed to go on for ever. Petri tested blood pressure, he put me through some kind of scanner, he checked my heart, tapped my knees, FLICKED MY EARLOBES, even measured my toes. I wondered about the HQ Manual and where I could find it. It had seemed quite straightforward to read a book and then escape. I hadn't realised I'd be going into a huge library floating thousands of feet above the ground and guarded by ninja librarians.

"So," Petri said at last, "and now, the final test."

He handed me a thin book and then emptied a bag on the table next to me. Springs and pieces of metal, screws and glass tubes rattled across the surface. I frowned. "Read the book and assemble this device," Petri said.

I nodded and flicked the pages of the book, soaking up every word in MILLISECONDS. I looked at the random pieces of metal and glass on the table and suddenly knew what each was for and where it went. In a few minutes, I had reassembled the device. It looked like a hat made of wire and strips of metal. Petri held it up. "Amazing," he said. "Just by reading that book, you were able to reassemble the Memory Eraser. Wonderful."

"Thanks," I said. "The knowledge doesn't seem to last, though, professor. It only stays in my head for about a day or so."

"Yes," Petri said. "I was able to talk to Professor von Gleitz, the man who invented the serum just before he died. He mentioned something about the knowledge only lasting twenty-four hours. Mind you, if you really want to learn something, you can read about and practise it just like anyone else."

I thought about Doctor Badd and the HQ Manual. I had an idea. "Do you want me to read something else? Any . . . manuals . . . or something like that?" I said, hopefully.

Petri blinked at me through his thick glasses. "No," he said. "That's proof enough."

I bit my lip. How was I going to get hold of the Headquarters User Manual? And even if I did get it, how was I going to escape? I sank back on the bed. The truth was, I couldn't get it and Anthony was **DOOMED!**

Chapter 10

10 - 153.1

SURVIVAL WITHOUT DIGESTIVES

P rofessor Petri looked at me and scratched his head. "You don't look very happy," he said. "Why not?"

"The truth is, professor, my mum's new boyfriend, Anthony, has been kidnapped by FART and they want me to come here and read the HQ Manual," I said.

"If you read that, then you'd have ALL THE SECRETS of the SLS Sky Library in your head," Professor Petri said, frowning. "That would never do."

"But what about Anthony?" I wailed. "Could you help me, professor?"

Petri's bushy white eyebrows shot up. "I couldn't possibly," he said. "The HQ Manual is top secret, to let anyone unauthorised read it would be a terrible breach of security.

It's a very sensitive document, that's why it's kept in the 'not for external loan' section!"

"Thanks Professor," I said, flicking a switch on the Memory Eraser and sticking it on his head. "You won't remember any of this; I've just set it to clear your memories of the last fifteen minutes."

The Professor began to say something but then the Memory Eraser bleeped and he **SLUMPED INTO HIS CHAIR**. Maybe Super Reading did have its advantages after all. I hurried down the corridor towards the main library room.

Unaware of my escape, Paige and Kazu were over on the other side of the room looking up at the screen on the wall. I could see a shadowy outline on the screen.

"Well done, Turner," the silhouette on the screen said. "You straightened out what was quite a dog-eared situation. The boy has Super Reader powers then?"

"It seems so, Carnegie," Paige said. "He's with Professor Petri undergoing tests now."

I slipped through the door and crept behind the nearest bookcase. The titles **SEEPED** into my mind as I sneaked alongside the shelves: *Defusing a Book Bomb Volume 1, Dewey Classification and Communication, SURVIVAL WITHOUT DIGESTIVES, Ninja Stealth By Kazu Tanaka*. I paused and flicked my way through Kazu's book then moved with my new ninja stealth towards the 'not for external loan' section.

I scanned the shelves, picking out a few more useful texts, *How to Fly a Mobile Library* and *Escapology for Beginners.*

"You mustn't let him out of your sight," Carnegie's voice boomed across the room. "We don't know where he's been . . ."

CHARMING, I thought.

"Initial investigations show that FART might have a sleeper agent in his school," Carnegie said. I froze and listened. "If they get hold of him, they might use his powers for their own ends. We have lost one branch library already. I suggest we erase his memory and return him to his home . . ."

My heart pounded. *ERASE MY MEMORY?*

"But he might have skills that could help us," Paige said. "I don't like taking away people's memories, Carnegie, it's not fair."

"I know you don't Paige," Carnegie said. "That's why I'm in charge. I know when it's wise to take a tough decision."

I stared around wildly. Where was this HQ Manual? I had to find it. Any minute now, they'd come looking for me and find Professor Petri. If they caught me, they'd wipe my mind and then I wouldn't be able to help Anthony!

"Carnegie," Kazu said. "We don't know the full extent of the boy's abilities yet and to erase his memories would waste the last gift that Professor von Gleitz left us. Could we at least spend some more time finding out what he's capable of? If we could synthesise the serum from his blood samples, who knows what we might achieve?"

I scurried along the bookshelves, searching and searching. *Where is it? Where is it?* The blood pulsed through my head. Sweat trickled down my back. At any moment, Kazu might turn around and spot me.

"Very well," Carnegie said. "I'll give you twenty-four hours to prove his value to the service but after that, we erase his memory and plant him back at home."

There! The HQ Manual sat on the shelf, white and untouched. I grabbed it and opened it, flicking through the pages as I scurried towards the lift. My head swam as I absorbed engine settings for keeping the Sky Library in the clouds, air conditioning, electrics, computer systems, alarms, how to keep the staffroom fridge clean, door locks, **UNBLOCKING THE TOILETS**, the security code for all library computer systems, which floor polish to use in the Sky Library, how to program the television. I soaked up all the information I could, even the small print at the back. Then I slammed the book shut, panting. It was the most stuff I'd crammed my head with ever and it made me dizzy!

The library door banged open and Professor Petri walked in still wearing the Mind Eraser. "Has anyone seen Kian?" he said. "He just seemed to vanish under my nose."

Paige looked in horror at the professor. "Why are you wearing the Mind Eraser, Petri?"

Petri frowned and put a hand to his head. "Am I? How odd," he said. Then his eyes widened. "*OH NO!*"

Kazu hit a computer button and sirens sounded all over the building. She leant into an intercom. "All staff, this is an emergency, be on the lookout for a boy, five foot six, slight build, light brown hair. Detain if spotted."

I could see the lift door to the landing pad above them. All I had to do was run from the bookshelves to the door but how could I get there without being spotted by Kazu? I needed a distraction. Closing my eyes, I trawled through my memories of the SLS HQ Manual. *That's it!* I thought. *Electrics!*

Creeping back along the bookshelves, I found a panel in the wall. *If my reading serves me correctly*, I thought, *I can pop this panel open*. The panel popped open to reveal a confusing spaghetti of wires and cables. *Now, the red ones for security and lights.* I tugged at the red cables, pulling them from their sockets. Sparks spat up into my face and for a moment, I thought I'd been electrocuted but then sirens went dead and the lights went out. *Excellent!* I thought in the gloom. *Now the purple wires for stabiliser rockets but leave the yellows for the lifts.* I pulled them out and the Sky Library began to *ROTATE*.

On the other side of the room, Paige and the professor fell to the floor with a *SQUEAK* as it moved beneath them. Kazu held her footing. "What's going on?" Carnegie cried but my meddling must have affected the sound system because he sounded like he'd inhaled a balloon full of helium. "Why is the room spinning?"

"Something's happened to the Sky Library's stabiliser rocket," Kazu said. "The whole building is twirling like a top!"

Trying to stay upright as the room whirled, I crouched by the bookshelf and then launched myself towards the lift door. I stabbed the button with my finger but then Kazu gave a shout and landed, cat-like, next to me.

"Stand away from that door, Kian Reader," she said. "You're under arrest."

MOBILE LIBRARIES ON ICE!

Taking a deep breath, I thought back to reading the Ninja Training book. Could that help me now? Reading the karate book hadn't helped against Chadwick but that time the knowledge had faded before I got to use it. I took up a defensive stance. The book said to use your enemy's power and speed against them. The book said I didn't have to be strong or big to do this.

Kazu looked confused. "Where did you learn those ninja moves?" she said.

"I'm a quick reader, remember?" I said, leaning back and pressing the lift button again. Kazu frowned. "I don't want to hurt you," she said.

"Then let me go," I said. "You're not going to erase my

memory, I need it, thank you very much!"

The door pinged open and Kazu leapt forwards. "Chapter three of your book," I yelled, grabbing her leg, "the Power Flight Conversion throw. *HEEEEYAAAAH!*" I used the power of her leap to spin her round and send her flying across the room.

"AAAAAAAAGH!" Kazu crashed into a pile of bookshelves. She jumped to her feet and immediately fell over again. "What have you done?" She tried to stand up again and slipped over.

I winced. I didn't want to actually hurt anyone. I felt bad about what I'd done but I had to save Anthony! "Sorry," I said. "That's the Non-Friction section, remember?" The Sky Library was spinning faster now. Some of the books from the Non-Friction Section whirled across the room to where Paige and Professor Petri were frantically trying to stay upright and get control of the building by punching commands into the computer.

I jumped into the lift and punched in the code:

335.216.

The lift lurched and took me up to the landing deck. My head swirled with information and the sickening movement of the building. The cold air that rushed in when the lift doors opened made me feel better but then I saw that the mobile library vans were starting to **SLIDE AROUND** the landing deck. Things were getting worse.

It was dark outside now and the floodlights gleamed off the roofs of the mobile libraries as they picked up speed, skating across the deck. I ran across to Paige Turner's van, tugging at the door as it slid slowly along. It was locked and I didn't have the key. "Oh no, oh no, oh no!"

I hurried to the next one as it glided by. My feet slithered under me as the floor shifted. It was like being on an ice rink. *Mobile libraries on ice!* I thought. *If I'm not careful, one of these vans will squish me.* This one was locked too.

A **SICKENING CRUNCH** told me that two vans had crashed into each other. I rolled out of the way of a bright red mobile library with a huge clown painted on the front and grabbed at the door of a third vehicle that passed me by.

"Yess!" I hissed. The keys hung in the ignition and the door was open. I threw myself in and tried to remember how to start the thing up.

The dashboard slid away, revealing the flight controls. Looking up, I saw two vans slithering across the deck towards me. I'd have to fly quickly if I was to avoid them.

"AAAAAH!" I yelled, slamming my foot down on the pedal. The rockets roared into life. The two mobile libraries grew **BIGGER** as they flew towards me, then I pulled the steering wheel back and flew up into the sky. My heart thumped against my ribs as the roofs of the vans disappeared beneath me. I'd only ever ridden a bike before and here I was steering a flying mobile library into the clouds. I glanced in the rear-view mirror and saw the Sky Library spinning, but it seemed to be slowing down.

I'd better get down to earth, I thought. But how? And where? I hadn't really paid much attention to where we'd flown. The Sky Library was up in the sky obviously, but it could've been over BIRMINGHAM OR LONDON OR MANCHESTER for all I knew.

I thought hard, sifting through my knowledge of the vehicle after reading the book from the library. "Aha!" I shouted and flicked a switch that said 'auto pilot.' A mechanical voice said, "Please set your destination." I typed 'Hinderton Central Library' into a keyboard close to the button.

The mobile library tilted slightly and descended into the clouds below. I sat back and blew out a long breath. All I had to do was get to the school by midnight. I looked at the on-board clock, it was eleven thirty. *How did it get so late?* I thought. But then Professor Petri's examination had taken ages, so had the flight up here *and* meeting Asif and Prissy. I wondered what they were doing and what they would say if they could see me now. I grinned but then thought of Mum. Was she worried? What if she'd phoned Dad? That wasn't a problem, Dad spent most of his time on the canal and his phone battery was always dead. Even when it wasn't, reception down at the canal side was rubbish. I felt that stab of guilt, all the same.

The lights of Hinderton appeared from beneath the blanket of cloud and, as I descended, they grew bigger. Even in the darkness, I could see the black strip of the canal that ran through the town's heart. Streetlights became clearer and more individual, other lights, from cars and traffic signals on the roads below grew brighter. Everything looked an orangey-yellow.

I flicked on the stealth button, making the van invisible and it slowly drifted down to the empty library carpark. With a HISS, the rockets died and the mobile library bumped to a halt. I threw open the door. Eleven forty-five. I had fifteen minutes to get to the school playground and meet Doctor Badd. If I ran, I could just make it.

Someone or something moved in the shadows by the library door. I didn't wait to see who or what it was, there wasn't time. My feet clattered on the pavement as I sprinted off down the street. The sound of my heavy footsteps echoed around me as I ran. Every now and then a lone car glided by, lit yellow by the streetlights.

Five minutes to go. My ragged breathing began to drown out the sound of my feet as running became harder. Shops turned into houses and soon I ran along the edge of the school playing field.

A large black shape squatted at the edge of the field and as I drew closer, I made out the rotor blades and dark silhouette of a helicopter. Doctor Badd was waiting.

"I've been waiting," Doctor Badd said, RUBBING HIS HANDS.

"Come here and recite the SLS HQ Manual to me . . ."

"Where's Anthony, Mum's New Boyfriend, first?" I demanded. Doctor Badd smiled and WAGGED HIS FINGER. "Ah! Very good young man, very good!" he said. "Bring out the prisoner!"

Badd's two identical heavies, both wearing sunglasses, pushed Anthony to the door of the helicopter. He was still tied up and he was grinning up at the night sky, like he didn't have a care in the world.

"What have you done to him?"

Doctor Badd smiled. "A temporary memory wipe," he said. "He is not harmed. He will remember nothing. Now come here and tell me what I want to know . . ."

I stepped forwards but, from nowhere, a dark figure sprang in front of me.

"That's far enough," Paige Turner said, holding a HUGE dictionary. "Nobody move or I throw the book at you!"

Chapter 12

12 - 364

IT'S ALWAYS THE CARETAKER!

Doctor Badd looked stunned. "What is the meaning of this?" he snapped. The two heavies dragged Anthony back into the helicopter.

"No!" I cried, jumping forwards. "I didn't know! She must have followed me."

"Too right I did, sonny," Paige said. "Did you think it would be so easy to escape from SLS HQ? We thought you were up to something."

"You mean you let me escape?" I said, staring in disbelief.

Paige Turner raised the book. "Kazu's forces are on their way Badd, you'd better come quietly."

"Never!" Badd snarled.

"Have it your own way," Paige said, heaving the book onto

her shoulder.

"Noooooo!"

THUMP!

"Aaaaaaargh!"

I blinked. Paige had vanished under two shadowy forms who dived on her from the darkness. The huge dictionary flew across the school playground and landed with a thud that **SHOOK THE EARTH.**

In the confusion, Badd leapt back into his helicopter.

"I'll give you one more chance, Kian Reader," he cried as the helicopter rose into the air. "You have twenty-four hours to find me and tell me what I need to know otherwise it's the curtains for Anthony, probably some venetian blinds too!"

"Er, boss," one of the heavies started to say.

"I know, I know! It's not *the* curtains!" Badd yelled. "He knows what I mean! **MWAHAHAHAHAHAHAHAHAHAHAHA!**" His voice faded as the helicopter vanished out of sight.

Paige Turner groaned and I span round to see Prissy and Asif, dressed in black. "You two!" I said. "What do think you're doing?"

"Helping you, of course," Prissy said. "You see, the moment you said you didn't want our help, I **VOWED** to help you. It's just the way I am."

"We followed you to the library but you didn't come out," Asif said. "We were really worried. We were going to break in and find you but then that Library Van appeared from nowhere in the carpark and you jumped out! Crazy."

"You see, Asif, Kian wasn't making it all up at all" Prissy snapped. "I told you we should believe him!"

"Erm, no you didn't," Asif said, frowning.

Before Prissy could argue, Paige groaned. "What happened?" she said. "Untie me right now!"

"It's okay," Asif said. "I've velcroed her hands and feet together. She's not going anywhere."

"Velcroed?" I said. "How?"

Asif grinned. "I have these straps with really strong Velcro on them," he explained. "They keep my leg splints on. I've got loads of spares, great for holding enemies!" he held up a bundle of rather grubby-looking straps. "It's my super power."

I hurried over to Paige, who glared at me through wonky glasses. "Let me go! I must stop Doctor Badd!" she snapped. "Kazu Tanaka's on her way, you know . . ."

Asif appeared at my side dragging the book. "This is really heavy," he said. "Hi, Mrs Turner!"

"Asif! You should be ashamed of yourself, accosting an elderly librarian and you a Wednesday Club Book Ambassador too!" Paige said. "I'LL HAVE YOUR LIBRARY CARD FOR THIS, young man!"

Asif looked sheepish. "Sorry Mrs Turner," he said. "I didn't know it was you and I didn't know you were a spy and I didn't know you weren't going to drop this book on Kian. Why is it so heavy?"

"It's a condensed book," Paige said. "Forty volumes squeezed into one book. It would have smashed the helicopter's rotor blades and stopped Badd from escaping, but *you* paid to that!"

"Come on," Prissy said. "We'd better get away if old Turner's pals are coming soon."

"You stay right where you are," Paige said wriggling to get free and failing. "You're under arrest for aiding an international criminal . . ."

"Well I don't think you're actually in the best position to arrest us," Prissy said, putting her hands on her hips.

"You mustn't let Badd know what's in the SLS HQ Manual!" Paige said, still struggling with the Velcro bands that Asif had put in place.

"Why not?" I asked.

"The Sky Library has the most **ADVANCED WEAPONRY** and technology in the world," she replied. "If he got control of the Sky Library, then the whole planet is threatened!"

"We could help you, Mrs Turner," Asif said. "We could be spies too!"

"I think you three have done enough damage already!" Paige snorted.

"Does the SLS ever go into space, Mrs Turner?" Asif asked.

"Only, I've always wanted to be an astronaut. Velcro was invented for astronauts and I'm very nifty with Velcro, as you can see..."

Paige Turner glared at Asif who realised his demonstration of his niftiness with Velcro wasn't exactly winning him any friends.

"We're wasting time," Prissy said. "Come on, let's get out of here."

They began to walk away. "Bye, Mrs Turner," Asif said. "See you next Wednesday."

"Come back here!" Paige yelled. "You know too much! **YOU NEED TO BE MEMORY ERASED!**"

I turned to look at her. "I'm going to rescue Anthony," I said. "And you won't stop me."

We hurried across the dark playground and suddenly, I felt tired. "Where can we go?" Asif asked.

"The canal," I said. "It's easier to think there."

"No," Prissy said.

"Why not?" I said, throwing my hands up in disbelief.

Prissy glanced around. "**DUNNO, BUT JUST NO.**"

"How about the library then?" Asif suggested.

"No," Prissy said. "Wait, I know, let's go down to the canal. It's easier to think there."

I shook my head. "Good idea, Prissy."

The banks of the canal were empty and it was **DEATHLY** quiet. They reminded me of Dad's sad face and I felt a stab of guilt.

If I was going to make things right, I needed to rescue Anthony. I told the others everything that had happened along the way. "How can I find Doctor Badd in twenty-four hours?"

"I dunno," Prissy shrugged. "But if you don't, then the information will fade and you won't have a second chance."

Asif stood up. "We need to do some **DETECTIVE** work," he said. "And luckily for you, mateys, I was born to be a detective."

"No you weren't, Asif," Prissy said. "And stop calling us 'mateys' or I'll poke you in the eye."

"Yes I was," Asif argued back. "And what's more —"

"Wait!" I said. "Asif is right. The first time I met Doctor Badd was in school. He measured my head and stuff and kept on saying, '*AHA!*'"

"What?" Prissy said.

"Sorry?" I replied.

"You said, *AHA!*"

"No! Doctor Badd said, '*AHA!*'"

Asif glanced round. "He's here?"

"*NO!*" I slapped my hands to my sides in frustration. "Listen! Doctor Badd was looking for someone who had been given the Super Reader Serum . . ."

"But to get into school, he must have had someone working for him on the inside," Asif said.

Prissy shrugged. "Nope," she said. "Still don't get it."

"You just weren't listening!" Asif said. "You can't just walk into a school and ask to measure children's heads."

"Of course you can't!"

"So a member of staff from the school must have let Doctor Badd in!" Asif said. "Someone on the inside is working for FART!"

"It's that **DINNER LADY**," Prissy said at last. "The one who hates me and always makes me go to the back of the queue."

"To be fair Prissy," I said. "You always try to push in at the front."

"**THE CARETAKER**, then," Prissy said. "It's always the caretaker! The caretaker in disguise!"

"We haven't got a caretaker," Asif pointed out.

Prissy scowled at him. "We have. He's called Mr Giles."

"He's not a caretaker, he's a site manager," Asif said, with a smug nod. "It says on his badge if you'd only read it!"

"The site manager, then!" Prissy snapped.

"Nope."

"Mrs Pilkins, the headteacher, Madame Sloof from French, Mr Jones," Prissy said. "Mr Hobson . . ."

"Prissy, you can't just name all the staff you don't like," I said.

"**PROFESSOR QUIRRELL!**" Prissy yelled, clapping her hands.

"He's not real, Prissy," I sighed, shaking my head.

"It's Mr Vestibule," Asif said in a small voice. "He's the one who sent you to see Doctor Badd, in the first place. **HE'S THE FART AGENT.**"

I felt a bit dizzy. "You're right," he said. "He's the one who was standing behind the Mayor on Saturday. He was with Doctor Badd!"

"Mr Vestibule, an agent of FART," Prissy giggled. "I love saying that, by the way."

"Well, it makes sense to me," I said. "He's always making reading boring and banging on about how important it is. What about that time he made you read all break time as a punishment, Asif?"

"That was a punishment?" Asif said, blinking in disbelief.

"Then **VESTIBULE IS OUR MAN**," Prissy said, narrowing her eyes.

"It's got to be him," Asif said. "So Mr Vestibule and Doctor Badd are in the area, closing down libraries and searching for this serum. Then they hypnotised Martin Marvello the famous, local, best-selling, award-winning children's author to steal the Reader Serum but you got it on your head instead."

I felt the blood drain from my face. "Oh no."

"What?" Prissy said, desperately trying to keep up.

"All that showing off in class yesterday," I said. "It just showed Mr Vestibule that I'd taken the serum. It was my fault that Anthony was kidnapped. If I hadn't been such a big head, they might have left me alone." I looked at Prissy and Asif. "And if I'd told you what was going on and trusted you two, then things mightn't be so bad now. I'm sorry."

An embarrassed silence fell over the three of them.

"Yeah, well, you can't help being a *NUMBSKULL*," Prissy said at last, punching me on the arm.

"Oww!" I hissed. "That hurt."

"You love it!" Prissy said, grinning.

"I don't," I muttered.

"Do!"

"Don't!"

"Stop!" Asif said. "Don't you realise what this means?"

Prissy's eyes glowed. "Yes," she said. "It means Mr Vestibule is the next link in the chain that leads to Dr Badd. It means our teacher has information we need. It means we're going to have to kidnap Mr Vestibule and *TORTURE* every last scrap of information out of him!"

THEY NIBBLE WITH EXTREME PREJUDICE

For the rest of the night, Asif and I stayed at Prissy's house. "I told my mum and dad it was a sleepover for Prissy's birthday," said Asif.

"I told *my* mum I was night fishing with my dad but she's going to go mad anyway!" I said. "Don't your parents mind you being out on a school night?"

"Nah," Asif said. "If I did it too much, they would, but they like me to have friends." He grinned over at Prissy. "Even friends like Prissy!"

"Oy!" Prissy snapped, SCOWLING AND SMILING AT THE SAME TIME, which was a bit disturbing.

Prissy lived in a big old townhouse not too far from the canal. It was tall and thin and had three floors. Prissy and her mum only really lived on the first two and they didn't seem too bothered about wallpaper and decoration. Posters of rock stars and UNICORNS, films and mountains plastered the walls. There were loads of books too, about Yoga and Transcendental Meditation and India and Ecology and MYSTICISM (whatever that is) and an old boy band called Take That (Prissy's mum was a big fan, apparently). Colourful blankets and throws covered all the furniture and there was a sweet, perfumy smell in the air. I thought about my house which was all neat and tidy with laminate floors and beige walls. Prissy's house was cooler.

Her mum had gone to bed, thinking we were all tucked up and sound asleep. Asif and I hurried off to one of the many unoccupied bedrooms and found blankets and sleeping bags. I didn't sleep well at all. Questions kept turning over in my mind. What did Doctor Badd want with the SLS HQ Manual? Was Mum okay? Was Anthony okay? How would they get Mr Vestibule tomorrow? AND TIME WAS TICKING AWAY. By ten p.m. tomorrow, I'd forget the contents of the manual.

I must have fallen asleep at some point because the next thing I knew, Prissy was looming over me, holding a hamster in each hand and kicking me in the thigh.

"Come on get up, we'll be late for school!" she said.

"What are you doing with them?" I groaned, sitting up. I felt a bit embarrassed sitting in a sleeping bag in just a T-shirt and boxers in front of Prissy.

"These," said Prissy, "are Cecil and Bertie, my **BATTLE HAMSTERS!**"

"Battle Hamsters," I repeated.

Asif leapt out of his sleeping bag in just his undies, showing no bashfulness at all. I'd seen his bare legs and all his scars before, he was very proud of them and used to frighten the Year One kids with them back in primary school. "Awesome," he said. "What can they do? Can they **RAM THE ENEMY WITH THEIR BONY SKULLS?** Or can they slash with their claws? Are they electrically charged?"

Prissy held them up. "They **NIBBLE**," Prissy said. "With extreme prejudice."

Asif frowned. "Why are they prejudiced?" he said. "Doesn't that mean like they're racist or something?"

Prissy shook her head. "Noooo," she said. "It means they are **TOTALLY DESTRUCTIVE** to the enemy. One glimpse of these bad boys ... erm ... hamsters and I'm telling you, old Vestibule will be pooing his pants and begging to tell us where Doctor Badd is!"

"Do people really do that when they're scared?" Asif said, pulling his school trousers on. "Poo their pants, I mean."

"Yes," Prissy said and she sounded so certain that I was a little bit worried.

"Er, can I get dressed?" I asked, hoping that Prissy would forget about the hamsters and leave them behind.

"Sure," Prissy said, grinning and nuzzling the hamsters.

"Cecil and Bertie don't mind, do you boys?"

I pulled the sleeping bag up to my neck. "I didn't really mean Cecil and Bertie," I said. "I meant YOU!"

"Oh," Prissy said, her face darkening. I could see her inner struggle. Being so oppositional was really hard work sometimes.

"Or maybe you could feed Cecil and Bertie *while* I get dressed," I said. "Or not. It's okay, really. It doesn't matter," I lied.

Prissy's face brightened. "Good idea," she said and hurried out of the room.

Prissy's mum was really tall and wore a long, multi-coloured dressing gown. She leant against the door frame watching us eat our Coco Pops, with a big smile on her face.

"You know I'm sure there were only two of you last night, Prissy," she said. "Where did this one spring from?"

"This is Kian," Prissy said, spraying Coco Pops all over the table. "He's a secret agent."

"Cool," Prissy's mum said. I smiled at her. Normally when adults said, 'cool' it sounded anything but 'cool.' Somehow, when Prissy's mum said it, it did sound 'cool.'

"Your mum's cool," Asif said as they hurried along the street to school.

"She's not, SHE'S A MONSTER," Prissy said, checking that Cedric and Bertie were safe in the bottom of her bag. "She was just being nice because you were there. Normally, I'm locked in the cellar and forced to do MATHS ALL NIGHT."

"Do you think it was wise to bring the hamsters?" I said.

"Yes," Prissy replied, not looking up.

"What are we going to do?" Asif said. "Are we going to get him at break or lunchtime?"

"I think after school is the only real chance we're going to have to get him," I said. "Which doesn't leave a lot of time for rescuing Anthony, but I can't see how we're going to get to him during the day."

As it turned out, we needn't have worried. School went its own sweet way as if nothing weird in the world had happened. We had assembly as if there weren't librarian spies, we went to Maths as if there wasn't an evil organisation called **FART** trying to stop everyone from reading and Chapman called us names just like he always did, not knowing that we were planning to kidnap and interrogate a teacher.

All morning, Prissy spent her time **WHISPERING** into her bag and feeding her hamsters sunflower seeds.

"Will you stop that?" I snapped as I walked past her desk in Maths. "People are beginning to think you're strange."

Prissy gave him a disbelieving look. "Kian," she said. "I think you've got me mixed up with someone who actually gives a stuff about what other people think."

"What are you doing anyway?" I asked her.

"Giving them a pep talk and feeding them up for the struggle to come," Prissy said, narrowing her eyes as if she could see a battle in the distance.

The lesson before lunchtime was English with Mr Vestibule. We were looking at **IRREGULAR VERBS** and had fifty exercises to complete in silence. I did them until my head swam. I looked over at Prissy who had made a hat out of the question paper. Asif had his head down and was eagerly writing.

Mr Vestibule didn't mention my absence, but he sat at his desk, staring at me and tapping his pen on the desk. **TAP, TAP, TAP**. Towards the end of the lesson he said, "Kian, Prissy and Asif, I'd like to see you at lunchtime."

I glanced across at Prissy again but she had her head stuck in her bag. Asif looked wide-eyed and pale.

The exercises on irregular verbs were collected in and the bell rang for dinner. Everyone piled out of the classroom except me, Asif and Prissy. Mr Vestibule stood up, closed the classroom door and pulled the roller blind over the window. Then he sat at his desk again and pulled out his phone, fiddling with the screen as he spoke.

"I believe you met a friend of mine, yesterday," he said, still looking at the phone.

I glanced at the others. Asif shook his head.

"Who, sir?" I said.

Mr Vestibule looked up. "Oh, **DON'T ACT DAFT**, Reader," he said. "Doctor Badd, you met Doctor Badd."

"Who sir?" I said. "Is he the man who measured my head?"

Mr Vestibule heaved a sigh. "I don't know what your game is Reader but he wants that information and I intend to get it for him. Now, look into the phone screen." Mr Vestibule lifted his phone to face us. I could see a **BLACK AND WHITE SWIRLING PATTERN** on the screen. It seemed to grow and fill my vision, turning and spinning. "Look deeper into my hypnophone, all of you. Let it take control."

It was amazing. I couldn't take my eyes off it. It filled the room. Slowly my mind began to feel numb, my breathing relaxed and I slumped in my seat. I knew Mr Vestibule had hypnotised me but I no longer cared. Perhaps if I told him everything, then all the trouble would be over and I could go fishing with Dad again. That would be nice. No more Doctor Badd, no more Anthony, just me and Dad, fishing. Nice and calm. Slowly, I slipped **DEEPER INTO MR VESTIBULE'S POWER**.

ANSWER ME IN A REALLY SQUEAKY VOICE

"I s that meant to be *doing* something?" Prissy said in a loud voice. "I mean it's a nice pattern but is it meant to be *hypnotising* me?"

I blinked, slowly coming around from the trance.

Mr Vestibule scowled at Prissy. "I might have known it wouldn't work on *you*, Prissy McBeef," he hissed. "You're so contrary, I would've been better telling you NOT to look at the screen."

"Yeah, well," Prissy said, rummaging in her bag. "It's too late now. Here, face the full wrath of my *BATTLE HAMSTERS!*" Prissy ran forwards and plonked Cecil and Bertie on Mr Vestibule's desk.

He frowned and looked up at her. "Your what?" he said.

"Erm, battle hamsters?" Prissy said. "Don't you find them terrifying?"

"No."

"Oh well," Prissy said, snatching Mr Vestibule's phone and **TURNING THE SCREEN TOWARDS HIM**. "Maybe this will convince you. Look deep into the screen Mr Vestibule."

"No, I . . . hey that's my phone," he said. "And that's . . . wow, that's a pretty pattern." I watched in amazement as Mr Vestibule's face slackened as he became more and more entranced by the hypnophone. "I . . . I . . ."

"Now Mr Vestibule," Prissy said. "You are under my power."

"I am under your power," Mr Vestibule said.

"You will do **ANYTHING** I say," Prissy said.

"I will do **ANYTHING** you say," Mr Vestibule repeated.

"And us! You'll do anything we say," I added.

"And you! I will do anything you say," Mr Vestibule said.

"I want you to imagine you're a ballerina," Prissy said. "The best in the world. Dance around the room."

Mr Vestibule lifted his chin and, with a smug smile on his face, began to hop and skip, throwing out his arms and bending. I grinned.

"This is cool," Asif said. "Do an Elvis impression, Mr Vestibule, sir."

Mr Vestibule started to **ROTATE HIS HIPS AND CURL HIS LIP**, whilst singing 'Hound Dog'. Asif laughed and clapped his hands.

"Now put the **WASTEPAPER BIN** on your head and go out into the school yard and shout 'I'm rubbish' at the top of your voice," Prissy said, "Oh! And go around kicking all the dinner ladies up the bum!"

"No!" I snapped. "Wait!"

Mr Vestibule stopped, wastepaper bin in hand.

"What're you doing?" Prissy said. "I was having fun!"

"We're not here to have fun," I reminded her. "We're here to find out where Doctor Badd is. We need to ask Vestibule some questions."

Prissy scowled. "Fair enough," she muttered. "Vestibule, you will answer our questions honestly."

"Do I kick the dinner ladies up the bum, after that?" he asked.

"No," I said. "Just answer our questions honestly."

He looked **A BIT DISAPPOINTED**. "I will answer your questions honestly," he said.

"Excuse me, Mr Vestibule, but where can we find Doctor Badd?" Asif said.

Vestibule stared into the wastepaper bin. "Doctor Badd is waiting in his mountain lair in the little-known, tiny Eastern European principality of Bolgradivia."

"Eastern Europe?" I groaned. "How are we going to get there?"

"The most common form of transport is by aeroplane," Vestibule said. "It takes two hours to fly there. There are few train links and no motorways."

"I wasn't asking *YOU*," I snapped. "It was a rhetorical question!"

"What does Doctor Badd want with Kian?" Prissy asked. "And answer me in a really squeaky voice."

"I don't know," Mr Vestibule squeaked. "He wanted Kian because of his Super Reader Powers but he did not tell me what he wanted Kian to do."

"Thank you," Prissy said. "Now do the Twist."

Mr Vestibule started dancing as if he was at a disco in the Sixties. "What are we going to do?" Asif said.

"I would take me to the Secret Library Service, to show that you can be trusted and get them to fly you there," Mr Vestibule squeaked, still in question-answering mode and still dancing.

They all stared at Mr Vestibule who carried on twisting next to his desk. "That's a brilliant idea," Asif said. "Why didn't we think of that?"

"Because you aren't very clever," Mr Vestibule said.

"But they'll erase our memories and send us home," I said. "I'll never rescue Anthony, then."

"Not if we tell them the truth," Asif said. "They'll have to rescue Anthony and if we program Mr Vestibule to only give the location of Doctor Badd if *we* can come, then Mrs Turner can't argue!"

"*STOP DANCING*," I said. "Okay this is what we're going to do. Mr Vestibule is going to take us on a trip right now. He will sign us out of school, take us to the library and we'll try to get the SLS to help us."

"And if they refuse to help us, we can use this," Prissy said, holding up the hypnophone. She leant over and whispered to Mr Vestibule, "You *are* TERRIFIED of my Battle Hamsters, by the way."

Mr Vestibule nodded, tugged at the knot of his tie and scanned the classroom for Cecil and Bertie. "Eek," he said.

A short while later, we stood in Hinderton Library at the check-out desk. Paige Turner did not look pleased to see us.

"YOU," she said. "I'm surprised you DARED show your face round here. As for you Asif, I'm very disappointed in you. If I wasn't so committed to reading for pleasure, I'd revoke your library card!"

Asif's face went bright red. "Sorry, Mrs Turner but I had to help my friend and we thought you were a baddie."

"We've brought you this," Prissy said pushing Mr Vestibule. "Tell Mrs Turner all about yourself, Vesty."

"My name is Egbert Tremain Vestibule, I am a FART agent masquerading as a teacher at Hinderton Academy," he squeaked. "I have been hypnotised by mere children and, were I not in a trance, would be highly embarrassed. Hamsters terrify me."

Paige suppressed a smile. "You've been having fun; I can see that."

I took a breath. "The thing is, Doctor Badd has taken my Mum's New Boyfriend prisoner and if I don't go there and tell Doctor Badd what he needs to know, then it's curtains for Anthony."

"Roller blinds too," Asif said.

"And wooden shutters," Prissy added, waggling her eyebrows.

"That's why we ran away from you," I said. "But Mr Vestibule knows the location of Doctor Badd's hideout and it's too far away to catch the bus so . . ."

"So you thought I'd take you there," Paige Turner said, frowning. "Well if you think I'm going to take a load of kids into a dangerous criminal's lair, you've got another thing coming. Come on, tell me where Doctor Badd is."

Mr Vestibule stood up straight. "I will only give the location to Kian, Prissy or Asif," he said. "They are my **SUPERIORS** and they **ROCK**."

I gave Prissy a pained looked. "You told him to say that?"

Asif grinned. "No, it was me."

Paige banged her fist on the counter. "Look," she snapped. "This isn't a game. It's dangerous. You could get hurt. Or worse."

"Well, Doctor Badd is expecting me, for one thing," I said. "So he won't be very happy if a load of SLS mobile libraries come flying over the horizon towards him. You're going to have to take me and you won't get the location without taking my friends. I suppose it depends on how badly you want

Doctor Badd."

Carrel Filler appeared from the office behind the counter. She'd obviously overheard everything. "Take them Paige," she said. "Kian's already proved he has brains. There aren't many children who can say they've disabled the Sky Library and escaped in a mobile library van. And those two overpowered you."

"That was sheer good luck," Paige snorted. "I didn't expect —"

"Exactly," Prissy said. "*Nobody* expects *us* to pose a threat, but look!" She whipped Cecil and Bertie from her bag and held them out like a pair of six-shooters. Mr Vestibule gave a **YELP** and cowered behind a newspaper stand.

Paige blinked at the two dangling hamsters. "Am I meant to feel intimidated?" she said.

"They're my Battle Hamsters," Prissy said. "Fear them."

"No," Paige replied.

"Please, Mrs Turner," I said. "I've been horrible to Anthony. He loves books and is always trying to get me reading. I can't just abandon him."

Paige's mouth twitched. She looked at Carrel and then back at me. "Always trying to get you to read, eh?" she said. "Loves books. Sounds like he's worth saving. Very well. Carrel, fire up the mobile library, **WE'RE GOING ON A MISSION!**"

Chapter 15

15 - 641.5

FOUR KILOS OF CARROTS, COFFEE? TOILET ROLL (EXTRA SOFT)

The mobile library **SOARED** into the sky as Asif and Prissy stared in disbelief at the view. "This is awesome," Prissy grinned and then realised she was enjoying herself so she scowled for a bit, just in case.

"It looks like candyfloss," Asif said, gaping at the clouds below.

"No it doesn't," Prissy muttered.

Paige glanced at me and nodded to the back of the van. "You might want to do a bit of reading," she said. "I particularly recommend *Infiltrating an Enemy Base* by J.Bond, *Disabling Security Systems* by P. Scott and *Escaping from Capture* by H. Houdini."

I nodded and hurried to the back of the mobile library to

find them. Carrel Filler, who was busy guarding Mr Vestibule, handed me the first text and I flicked through it.

"Don't worry," she said. "We'll get your mum's new boyfriend back safe and sound."

"Thanks," I said. I thought about Anthony, with his **RUBBISH JOKES** and the way he always tried to impress or please people. I felt guilty. "My dad says that he makes my mum happy."

"How long has he known your mum?" Carrel asked.

"Well, he's been living with us for five years and . . ."

Carrel's eyebrows shot up. "He's hardly a 'new boyfriend' then, is he?" she said.

I felt my cheeks colour. "No," I said. "He's been around for quite a while, I suppose."

"Almost half your life," Carrel said.

"Yes," I admitted. "I suppose I always called him 'Mum's New Boyfriend' to make him seem kind of temporary, not important." I looked up at Carrel. "It's a bit mean, really, isn't it?"

Carrel smiled at me. "Don't worry, we'll rescue him!"

"Hey, Mr Vestibule," Prissy called to the back of the Van. "Do the **I'M A LITTLE TEAPOT** song, in a Bart Simpson voice!"

"This is going to be a long journey," I said. Carrel nodded.

The mobile library flew across green fields and then the land gave way to sea and then land again. From time-to-time, I could see a patchwork of fields, green and brown, divided up by the sharp lines of railways or motorways. Sometimes a river would snake around the land or a town would cluster below turning the green to grey or black. Mountains grew, small mounds at first but then they became white with snow and I saw the **SHARPNESS** of the peaks.

"It won't be long now," Paige said. "Does everyone know the plan? Kian, you're going to have to take over the wheel soon. Can you still remember?"

"I can," I said, thinking hard. "It's all still there."

"Good," Paige said. "We'll hide in the mobile library, while you distract Doctor Badd by telling him **USELESS** things about SLS HQ. It's essential that you don't give him any sensitive information, just give him trivia, dimensions of the landing pad, thickness of windows, that sort of thing. We'll leave Mr Vestibule tied up here, sneak out and locate Anthony, then we can arrest Badd, destroy his base and be back in time for tea."

"A piece of cake," Prissy said. "Time to check the Battle Hamsters are ready for action!"

"You know, there aren't many people who are *actually* scared of hamsters," Paige said. "And they aren't really that fierce."

"Mr Vestibule fears them," Prissy said.

"Only cos you hypnotised him into being afraid of hamsters," I said. Mr Vestibule gave a **SMALL WHIMPER** from the back of the van.

"Well, just in case the hamsters don't have the impact you hope for," Paige said. "I have back-up," she said. "Kazu and her ninja librarians are shadowing us from a distance. If we aren't out of there in twenty minutes, they'll come and get us."

"That's comforting to know," I said, eyeing Prissy's Battle Hamsters.

A light on the dashboard began to flash. "Here we go," Paige said. "FART are trying to communicate with us. Places everyone!"

"Come on, Prissy," Asif said. "Time to hide in the back. I'll be invisible. I was *born* invisible."

"No you weren't," Prissy said.

"Yes I was."

"It doesn't even make sense. If you were born invisible how would the midwife be able to see you?"

"They had infrared goggles on . . ."

I ignored the bickering pair and slid into the seat that Paige had just jumped out of. Everyone else crouched behind bean bags and bookshelves. Asif threw a blanket over his head and sat in the middle of the floor.

I pressed the flashing button and Doctor Badd's CHIN AND CHEST appeared on a screen in front of him. "So, it is you, Kian Reader," he said. "Well done . . ."

"Er, boss," said a voice behind him. "You're not quite in shot."

"Doh!" Badd yelled and crouched down, revealing his grey face and yellow-toothed grin. "So it is you, Kian Reader," he said again. "Well done. I see you managed to steal an SLS mobile library. I'm impressed. One thing puzzles me, though."

"What's that?" I said, trying to sound as casual as possible.

"Why is your friend Asif with you?"

"What?" I said, glancing behind me and sounding genuinely surprised.

Asif scowled at Doctor Badd. "I was **MEANT** to be invisible," Asif said.

"Obviously you weren't," Doctor Badd chuckled. His face suddenly went serious. "This better hadn't be some kind of hopeless attempt at a trick, Reader. Or it's the curtains for your precious Anthony."

"No!" I said. "It's not! He . . . er . . . he was asleep in the mobile library when I stole it. I didn't know."

Doctor Badd came so close to the screen that I almost imagined I could **SMELL THE DOCTOR'S BREATH**. "It is of no concern," Doctor Badd said. "We can deal with him when you land. Follow these instructions and I will see you in a few minutes." Badd held up a sheet of paper with something written on it.

I frowned. "Four kilos of carrots? Coffee? Toilet roll (extra soft)?" I read aloud. "What's that all about?"

"Curses!" Badd hissed, crumpling up the paper. "That is my **SHOPPING LIST**. Here is the list of coordinates you need to reach my mountain-top base." He held up another sheet and I read the coordinates on it.

"I'll see you in a moment," I said and switched off the screen.

Asif sidled forwards. "What're we going to do?" he said. "Badd is going to 'deal' with me. That can't be good."

I grinned. "Don't worry, you were *born* brave, right?"

"I'm not sure," Asif said. "I think we might find out if scared people REALLY poo their pants with fear soon!"

The clouds parted and there, clinging to a sharp mountain peak was the darkest, most hideous building I had ever seen. It looked like a fairy castle gone bad. Black, tiled towers pointed jaggedly up at the sky and every angle of the walls looked impossibly crooked. A landing strip stretched out from the main gate, just daring them to land.

"Well, we can't back out now," I said. "Fasten your seat belts, we're going in."

Chapter 16

16 - 690

A BIGGER FART THAN YOU CAN EVER IMAGINE!

Doctor Badd stood on the runway, flanked by an army of identical-looking heavies with guns, waiting for us as I brought the mobile library to a halt.

"Welcome, welcome, to Castle Badd!" He yelled, clapping his gloved hands together as me and Asif climbed out of the van. "Come with me and together we will make history!"

"Ooh, I like History," Asif said, brightening up.

Badd stopped, turned round and frowned at Asif. "Hmm," he said. "I had forgotten about you." He clicked his fingers (which is almost impossible when you're WEARING GLOVES, so I was quite impressed). "Put this boy with the other prisoner and bring them to the control room."

Two huge, bald men, still wearing sunglasses, still dressed in black, grabbed Asif. "Let me go," Asif said, trying to wriggle free. "You'll be sorry. I was *born* to kill, you know!"

"Don't worry, Kian," Doctor Badd said, with a crooked smile. "He will be quite safe as long as you do as I tell you."

Doctor Badd led me across the runway and through an enormous gate. I shivered. It felt like I was walking into the open mouth of a HUGE MONSTER. Gargoyles studded the walls and the black brickwork gave the whole place a dismal, gloomy feel.

"Nice place you've got," I said, trying to sound sarcastic and brave.

Doctor Badd gave another grin. "Thank you," he said. "Castle Badd has been in my family for generations. Over the centuries, the Badd's have tried to break beyond the borders of this tiny, mountainous country but to no avail. Until now!" He stopped and punched the air. "Ow! MIND WHERE YOU'RE WALKING, fool!" Badd said.

"Sorry," I muttered. "If you hadn't STOPPED so suddenly, I wouldn't have walked into you!"

"I was being dramatic!" Badd said and then walked on muttering. "What's the point of being a maniacal criminal genius if you can't be dramatic?"

We crossed a cobbled courtyard and entered the keep at the centre of the castle. Inside, the character of the castle changed completely. It felt more like a laboratory than a medieval building. The walls were smooth white and the floors metal. Cameras clung to the ceiling, scanning our every move.

Every now and then, we passed a door and I could see white-coated scientists mixing chemicals or twiddling dials on complicated-looking machinery inside the rooms.

"This is the **NERVE-CENTRE** of my operations," Badd said.

"Wow," I said. "FART HQ"

Doctor Badd laughed and shook his head. "You think this is FART HQ? No, no, no, my friend. FART HQ is much bigger than this and many, many miles away."

I frowned. "But I thought you were the **HEAD FART**," I said.

For a split second, anger and disappointment flashed across Badd's face. "No," he said. "There is another. **A BIGGER FART** boss than me. I said to the committee who decides who's boss, 'put me in charge and I will make **FART HUGE**. The FART I have in mind is a bigger FART than you can ever imagine!' They just laughed."

"I bet they did," I muttered.

Badd narrowed his eyes. "But once I have the contents of the SLS HQ Manual," he said. "I will show them. It will be they who come to me, on bended knee. 'Oh mighty Doctor Badd, make FART huge, they'll say. Show us your vision. Show us how big FART can be!"

I bit my tongue and tried to blink away the tears. "Amazing,"

I said. "So with you in charge, the world would experience a bigger, more powerful FART than ever before?"

We entered a room lined with computers and screens. Doctor Badd gave me a sidelong glance. "I think you are being silly," he said. "Now, sit in this chair!"

Badd pushed me down into a large, black leather chair.

"I want you to tell me everything you can about SLS HQ," Badd said, steepling his fingers and staring over them at me.

"Well," I said. "It has eight drink vending machines. Two are for cold drinks and the rest are for hot. The hot ones serve seven types of coffee, tea, hot chocolate and chicken soup. The soup is the least favourite . . ."

"I need something more useful," Doctor Badd began.

"The toilets are very environmentally friendly and flush using a minimal amount of water. You might wonder what happens to all the . . . er . . . waste. Imagine if it was just sprayed into the sky so it rained down on people's heads, that wouldn't be very good. In fact, it's stored in tanks and —"

"Enough!" Doctor Badd snapped. "I know what you are doing, Kian Reader, but your time is up! Now think hard. I want you to recite the SLS Master Computer Security Code. It is just eight little digits. That's all I need. I don't need to know about VENDING MACHINES OR TOILETS . . ."

"The SLS HQ has a brilliant swimming pool you know," I said. "With a wave machine and everything . . ."

"Really?" Badd said, his eyebrows shooting up in surprise. "I thought those pesky librarians were more interested in books than swimming . . ."

"They have a jacuzzi too," I said. "And a sauna room."

"A sauna room, fancy that," Doctor Badd stared off into the distance, lost in a daydream about SLS saunas for a second, then shook his head. "All very lovely, Kian Reader," he snapped. "But I'll have the code now, if you please!"

"I don't know what code you mean!" I said, trying to avoid Doctor Badd's piercing gaze.

"I'm getting bored now," Badd said. He turned to a guard. "Bring the prisoners in."

Anthony and Asif were pushed in at gunpoint and sat in chairs. Anthony still looked dazed but Asif looked pale and worried. "Don't tell them anything, Kian," he said.

"You do have that choice, Kian Reader," Doctor Badd said, twiddling his thumbs around each other. "But if you choose to remain silent then Anthony and your dear friend Asif will suffer a slow, messy and embarrassing death.

"Tell him EVERYTHING he needs to know, Kian," Asif said.

I looked at Anthony and Asif. *Where are Paige and the others?* I thought. "I could tell you the combination of the custard cream safe," I said. "Did you even know they had a safe just for custard creams?"

Doctor Badd looked hard at me, almost as if he was reading

my thoughts. "You think I'm stupid? You've been trying to buy time," Badd said slowly. "There is someone else here! Guards! Quickly, search the castle, arrest anyone —"

"Anyone, boss?" one guard said. "Like each other?"

Badd **STAMPED** his foot. "No!" he shouted. "Let me finish my sentences! Arrest anyone who isn't a member of FART personnel!"

"You're imagining things!" Asif said. "There was only me and Kian. The others weren't there."

"The others," Badd said, giving an evil smile.

"Oh, I shouldn't have said that should I?" Asif mumbled.

"No," I said.

"Enough!" Doctor Badd said, leaning over me. "Tell me the codes now or it is the curtains for your friend."

Before I could reply, a guard came **CRASHING** through the door and landed, unconscious at Badd's feet. Paige Turner and Carrel Filler sprang in after him.

"Okay, Badd, the game's up," Paige said. "Surrender, now!"

Doctor Badd let out an evil laugh. "Mwhahahaha!" He laughed, evilly. "Do you really think it would be that easy to defeat me?" He clapped his hands and guards appeared from behind them, some jumped down from vents in the ceilings, others sprang from out of cupboards in the walls. Soon the room was full of identical heavies, dressed in black leather and wearing sunglasses. "Even if you did get to me," Badd said. "My men would cut your friends down. Face it, it is you who are defeated, and it is you who will have to surrender! MWAHAHAHAHAHAHA!"

IT'S NOT A PLACE, IT'S A SOUND EFFECT.

I looked in despair at the row of my friends all tied to chairs. Doctor Badd stood grinning like the CAT THAT HAD GOT THE CREAM. *Or the rat that had got the cheese*, I thought.

"So," Badd said, stroking his chin as if he was deep in thought. "Where were we? Oh! Yes! Kian was just about to give me the SLS Master Computer Security Code."

"Don't tell him Kian!" Prissy shouted.

Asif leant over and whispered in her ear. "He did say something before about us suffering a slow, messy and embarrassing death."

"Tell him *EVERYTHING*, Kian!" Prissy said.

I glanced around the room for anything that might help me. The guards had backed away and most had left the room.

Sitting on a bookshelf in the far corner of the room was a huge file. The file looked heavy and was covered in black leather. It had 'BADD FART HQ MANUAL' written on it.

I wonder, I thought. "Okay," I said. "The code you want is 56830172."

"Kian, no!" Paige gasped. "You've just handed him a super-weapon!"

Doctor Badd hurried over to a computer console and tapped in the numbers I'd told him. "**EXCELLENT!**" he said, clapping his hands. "I'm in!"

"What are you on about?" I said. "How can one number be a super weapon?"

"With that code, I have just hacked into every SLS computer in the world!" Badd said, beaming. "Why don't you tell him, Paige?"

Paige shook her head, sadly. "The Secret Library Service is an international organisation. It operates all over the world," she said. "But the need for secrecy is essential if we are to remain an effective fighting force. Every library in the world has an SLS safe room, stocked with weapons, listening devices, rations, equipment, everything you might need. Including a computer."

"So?" I said frowning.

Paige sighed. "Every SLS safe room computer has a self-destruct program. In the event of discovery, the SLS agent was to clear the library and destroy the safe room."

"*KABOOM!*" Badd said, clapping his hands.

"Kaboom?" Prissy said. "Where's that?"

"It's not a place, you fool!" Badd said. "It was a sound effect."

"What like onomatopoeia?" Prissy said. I frowned. What was Prissy up to? Normally, she'd be scowling away at being called a fool. And she'd NEVER ADMIT to knowing a word like onomatopoeia.

"No! Like, *KABOOM!*" Badd growled. "It was meant to be the sound of a library blowing sky high to the clouds!"

"Oh," Prissy said, looking unimpressed and glancing over at Asif.

"Now I have control of every SLS computer," Badd said, smiling wickedly. "With one press of a button, I can blow up ALL THE LIBRARIES IN THE WORLD! And all the SLS agents in them!"

"But you can't!" Carrel Filler gasped. "Those libraries will be full of innocent people!"

"They will be an example of the true power of Doctor Badd," Badd laughed. "Without libraries, mankind will once more fall into the dark ages of ignorance! Without the civilising influence of the librarian, FART will take over the world and I will become its leader!"

"Couldn't we just use the internet?" I said.

Paige glared at me. "How do you know what to look for? Where to look for it?" she snapped. "How do you look for different ideas about what it is you're looking for? How do you know what you've found out about is true or verified and not the opinions of some wild-eyed, rambling, conspiracy theorist locked in a bunker somewhere in Arizona? How about fiction and picture books?"

Doctor Badd's eyes shone. "Believe me, Kian Reader, without librarians, the world is doomed!" he said. "Doomed to be ruled by me! *MWAAHAHAHAHAHAHAHA!*"

Prissy jumped up, snapping her ropes as if they were made of cotton. "You're a bit *BONKERS*," she said. "I quite like that as a rule, but you're a bit *too* bonkers!"

Asif slithered out of his ropes too. "I think you're a bit bonkers too," he said. "But I don't like it at all."

Doctor Badd looked stunned for a second. "How did you escape?" he said.

"I was born escaping from things!" Asif said.

"That is kind of true," Prissy said, pulling a face and shuddering.

Doctor Badd groaned. "I wish I'd never asked," he said. "Never mind, guards! *KILL THEM!*"

Badd leant forwards and pressed the key on the computer, the key that would destroy every library in the world. Without thinking, I launched myself out of my chair and *RUGBY TACKLED DOCTOR BADD TO THE GROUND.*

But it was too late. "COUNTDOWN INITIATED.

SIXTY SECONDS UNTIL TOTAL DESTRUCTION OF

SLS LIBRARIES!" The computer announced over the HQ sound system.

"Countdown?" Badd yelled. "Why does there have to be a countdown?"

"It's more exciting boss," said a guard as he made a grab for Prissy and managed to fall headlong against the desk.

Meanwhile, other guards were chasing Prissy and Asif around the room, tripping over chairs and each other, as the two children ducked and weaved. Suddenly, Paige leapt to her feet, free of her ropes, followed closely by Carrel. I frowned. How did they escape so easily? Then I noticed Cecil and Bertie still gnawing at the ends of the ropes. So they were some use after all!

"*HEEEEYA!*" Paige yelled, knocking three heavies to the ground with one kick. "*HEEEEYA!*" Carrel took out two guards and threw a third into two others.

"FORTY SECONDS UNTIL TOTAL DESTRUCTION OF SLS LIBRARIES!"

I sat on Doctor Badd's chest, pinning him. "Prissy!" I called and nodded over to the BADD FART HQ MANUAL that stood on the shelf in the corner.

Prissy did a flip over two guards, landed by the shelf and reached up for the folder. "I can't get it!" she moaned. "It's too high!"

A guard closed in on her and she grabbed a wheeled chair, sending it **SPINNING** into him. Then she jumped onto the guard's head and grabbed the shelf, pulling the whole thing off the wall.

"THIRTY SECONDS UNTIL TOTAL DESTRUCTION OF SLS LIBRARIES!"

"Guards, get this idiot off me!" Badd yelled. A guard grabbed me by the arm just as Prissy threw the folder across the room. It hit the guard with a loud clunk and he collapsed to the floor. I snatched up the BADD FART HQ MANUAL but Doctor Badd loomed over me. "I've got you now," Badd snarled.

"TWENTY SECONDS UNTIL TOTAL DESTRUCTION OF SLS LIBRARIES!"

I looked down at the heavy file and then back at Badd. Just as the Doctor closed in, I swung the file, **BAM**, smacking Badd across the head. Badd stumbled and fell to the floor.

Without waiting to see if Badd was out cold, I flicked through the BADD FART HQ MANUAL, soaking up as much information as I could. My eyes widened as I read but I didn't have time to tell anyone what I had learnt.

"TEN SECONDS UNTIL TOTAL DESTRUCTION OF SLS LIBRARIES!"

Instead, I hurried over to the computer Badd had used to hack into the SLS system. "I think I can stop it!" I yelled.

"NINE, EIGHT, SEVEN, SIX, FIVE."

"Emergency override code," I muttered, tapping in the numbers I'd learnt from the BADD FART HQ MANUAL.

Nothing happened.

"FOUR, THREE . . ."

I tapped them in again, more carefully this time.

"THREE AND A BIT, TWO . . . ONE . . . BOOM! ONLY KIDDING. TOTAL DESTRUCTION OF SLS LIBRARIES ABORTED. IT'S OVER, YOU CAN RELAX, PEOPLE."

I quickly typed in the SLS Master Computer Security Code and changed it to a random sequence of numbers with my eyes closed. "There!" I said. "Now nobody can hack into the SLS computers for a while at least!"

Doctor Badd stood over me. "What have you done?" he snarled. "You have FOILED MY PLAN!"

A muffled explosion somewhere outside made him turn.

"That's the least of your problems, Badd," Paige Turner said. "The SLS Ninja Force are here to tear your castle apart!"

"Curse you!" Badd yelled. He pushed me out of the way and slammed his hand down on a huge red button next to the computer. "If I go, then you all go with me."

"HERE WE GO AGAIN!" said the computer.

"SIXTY SECONDS UNTIL TOTAL DESTRUCTION OF CASTLE BADD!"

Doctor Badd stood, looking from me to Paige. "This is a bit awkward," he said, filling the awkward silence. "Never really thought what I'd do whilst waiting for my castle to explode into a million fragments. Why does there always have to be a countdown?"

I looked at Prissy and Prissy looked at Asif who looked at Carrel who looked at Paige.

"I know what we can do," I said. *"RUUUUUUUUUUNNNNNN!"*

Chapter 18

18 - 662.0

I MUST KILL PAIGE TURNER

"FIFTY SECONDS UNTIL TOTAL DESTRUCTION OF CASTLE BADD!"

I grabbed hold of Anthony's hand and dragged him across the room towards the door. Paige and Carrel led the way and Prissy and Asif helped push Anthony along. Many of the guards ran ahead of us or chased behind, more interested in escape than capturing us.

"Run, you fools!" Doctor Badd laughed behind them. "You'll never escape in time!"

"Neither will you," Prissy yelled back at him.

"What?" he said. "Good point! *WAIT FOR ME. HEEEELP!*" Elbowing three of his own guards out of the way, Badd sprinted after us.

"FORTY SECONDS UNTIL TOTAL DESTRUCTION OF CASTLE BADD!"

My breath sounded ragged and my heart pounded as I pulled Anthony along through rooms and down corridors. Anthony still just smiled and stared around as if he was on a sight-seeing holiday.

"There's the door to the courtyard!" Paige shouted.

A figure LOOMED out of nowhere and blocked the exit. "I must kill Paige Turner," it said.

"It's Martin Marvello the famous, local, best-selling, award-winning children's author!" Asif panted. "That's all we need!"

"I wondered where he'd wandered off to," Paige said. "Out of the way, Martin! Now's not the time."

"I must kill Paige Turner!"

"THIRTY SECONDS UNTIL TOTAL DESTRUCTION OF CASTLE BADD!"

"Oh, blow this," Carrel Filler said, ducking under Martin Marvello's arm and THROWING HIM ONTO THE FLOOR.

"I must ... ooof!" Martin Marvello said. Carrel kicked the gun down the corridor and pulled Martin's arms behind his back.

Asif grabbed one of his Velcro strips and bound Martin Marvello's arms together, then they pushed him out into the courtyard.

"TWENTY SECONDS UNTIL TOTAL DESTRUCTION OF CASTLE BADD!"

Outside the keep, a battle raged. Mobile libraries hovered, FART heavies fired guns but whirling ninja's in black were taking them down all over the castle.

BOOM! A tower exploded over to our right.

DAKKA, DAKKA, DAKKA, DAKKA! Machine guns fired to our left.

KEEyA, KEEyA, KEEyAAAAAAAAAGH! A seagull exploded into flames and landed, a roasted carcass at Asif's feet. "Yuck," Asif said.

Kazu Tanaka slithered down a rope from a mobile and landed in front of us. "Pull your librarians back, Kazu," Paige said. "The whole place is going to **BLOW!**"

"TEN SECONDS UNTIL TOTAL DESTRUCTION OF CASTLE BADD!"

Doctor Badd emerged from the doorway of the keep, pushed Paige and Carrel out of the way and **SCURRIED** across the courtyard into one of the towers. I started after him but Carrel grabbed my shoulder.

"There's no time!" She yelled as more ropes dropped from the mobile library van above us.

"FIVE SECONDS UNTIL TOTAL DESTRUCTION OF CASTLE BADD!"

We all clipped ropes around our waists, I fixed Anthony's and Prissy saw to Martin Marvello's and the mobile library took off without winching us up. Once again my tummy

RACED DOWN TO MY BOOTS and back up again.

"THREE, TWO, ONE . . . NOT JOKING THIS TIME!"

A deep rumble shook the air around Castle Badd. The rumble grew into a roar and the roar became a bellow of explosive rage as flames burst from the heart of the castle.

KABOOOOOOOM!

I hugged the rope that dangled me above the destruction below and squeezed my eyes tight shut. The explosion filled my ears, blotting out the sound of the mobile library engines. The cold air quickly became warm, then hot, SCORCHING my eyebrows and taking my breath away. Small stones and chunks of wood bounced off my legs and when I opened my eyes, Castle Badd was a PILE OF RUBBLE sliding down the mountain in a cloud of dust and smoke.

But a small red bubble-shaped vehicle, a tiny aircraft or rocket zoomed out of the destruction and I knew that Doctor Badd lived to fight another day!

"You might have won today," Doctor Badd's voice drifted across the mountains. "But I'll be back to have my revenge, Kian Reader!"

Slowly the winches began to haul me and the others up until

Kazu dragged us inside what turned out to be Paige Turner's mobile library.

"Welcome back everyone," Mr Vestibule said, tied up in the back of the van. "D-did the hamsters make it?"

I slumped back into a seat and looked across at Anthony who still **GRINNED LIKE A BUFFOON** at everyone. Prissy sat next to Asif, stroking Cecil and Bertie. Carrel looked tired and ash smudged her face but she looked unhurt. Martin Marvello wrestled feebly with the bands that held him and whispered. "I must kill . . . Paige Turner . . ."

"Oh be quiet Martin!" Paige Turner said. "Thank you for rescuing my mobile library, Kazu."

"You're welcome, Paige," Kazu said. "When I saw it on the ground, I suspected it might have Mr V in it, so I had one of my operatives take it up into the sky."

"Well, we did it. Well done everyone," Paige said, blowing a stray strand of hair out of her eyes. "Another threat from FART stopped in its tracks."

"We certainly did," Prissy giggled. "We stopped **ONE HELL OF A FART** plot going down there."

"**A REALLY BIG ONE**," Asif said, smirking.

Prissy frowned at Asif. "How did you get free?" she asked. "Cecil and Bertie didn't nibble your ropes!"

"Escapology by H. Houdini," Asif said.

My eyes widened. "You mean you've got **SUPER READER**

POWERS LIKE ME?'

"No, Kian," Asif said. "I just *TRIED REALLY HARD TO READ THE BOOK AND REMEMBER IT*. It is possible you know! Anyway, I'm skinnier than you lot and having no thumbs meant I could slide my hands out of the rope easily."

"Wow!" I said, genuinely impressed.

"You see, Kian," Asif said. "You don't have to have superpowers to be useful and resourceful! And one day I'm going to be an astronaut!"

"So, a quick call to the Sky Library," Paige said. "Erase all your memories and you can all go back to being ordinary students with no knowledge of FART or the SLS or anything!"

"*WHAT? NO!*" I yelled. "I don't want my memories erased!"

Carrel smirked. "I thought you hated being a Super Reader."

I felt my face redden. "No, not really. It has its uses," I said. "But me, Prissy and Asif have been through a lot. They're my real friends. I don't want that wiped out."

"Cor!" Asif said. "Thanks, matey!"

"Whatever," Prissy said, rolling her eyes.

"And what about Anthony?" I said. "I don't want to go back to hating him!"

Paige raised her eyebrows and smiled. "We have changed our tune, haven't we?" she said. "If it were up to me, I'd leave you, but it's not up to me. It's up to Carnegie. He's responsible for the whole SLS. He'll decide and to be honest, he's not as soft-hearted as I am."

I sank back into my chair and listened to the roar of the mobile library's rockets taking us closer and closer to forgetfulness. WE WERE DOOMED!

Chapter 19

19 - 792.8

I CAN'T DO FRIDAYS, IT'S TAP-DANCING

We travelled back to the Sky Library in silence. All the way, I tried to think up a plan to escape but I couldn't take Anthony back to Mum with a **DOZY GRIN** like that. Plus, the SLS knew who I was and where I went to school. They could pounce on me at any time. I had to face facts, I was doomed.

"Forgetting this adventure won't be all bad," Asif said, trying to convince himself as much as us. "I mean, it was a bit scary, and I'd happily not remember Doctor Badd's ugly face!"

"Speak for yourself," Prissy said. "I never want to forget any of it and I'm **NOT** going to."

The Sky Library appeared out of the clouds. I could see the other mobile libraries belonging to Kazu's ninjas already parked on the landing deck. Figures scurried around refuelling and repairing the vehicles. Paige led us across the deck and soon we were being shepherded into the great library room. A dark silhouette of a man filled the big screen on the wall. We stood in front of the screen and I felt tiny and helpless.

"My name is Carnegie," said the figure. "Head of the Secret Library Service."

"Hi," Prissy said. Everyone else kept quiet.

"We brought them back as you ordered, Carnegie," Paige said. "What do you want us to do with them?"

"A memory erase should do it," Carnegie said. "We're very grateful to you, Kian, Prissy and Asif but I'm sure you will appreciate, a secret organisation like ours can't allow you to keep your memories of it . . ."

"But without us, the SLS wouldn't exist anymore," I said. "And we saved the world. I don't want my memories erased."

"I know, son," Carnegie said. "But sometimes, for the good of everyone, you have to make a sacrifice."

"Well, you're not erasing my memory," Prissy said.

"Thing is, Carnegie," Asif said. "If it wasn't for us, you wouldn't have known about Doctor Badd's plan and I think we were pretty good agents. In fact, I was born to be a secret agent. You should recruit us."

Carnegie's head shook and I wondered if he was laughing at us. Anger bubbled up inside me. "Listen, Carnegie," I said.

"We risked our lives for you. I didn't want to have this Super Reader power but I have. So why not use it for the good of mankind? Besides, you may be interested to know that FART have other plans and inventions. I read the BADD FART HQ MANUAL and I can give you that information. If you erase my memory, you'll lose it. Plus, Doctor Badd said he would have his revenge. What if he comes back and we don't remember him? At least if we keep our memories, we'll be watching for his return!"

"He's got a point, Carnegie," Carrel said, giving me a jump. "They all proved themselves to be capable agents. Kian disabled the Sky Library."

"We let him . . ." Carnegie began.

"We went easy on him," Paige corrected. "And he really caused trouble for us. I suspect he might have got away even if we'd really tried to stop him."

"And these two proved their worth," Carrel pointed to Prissy and Asif.

Prissy whipped out Cecil and Bertie from behind her back. "*BATTLE HAMSTERS!*" she declared.

Everyone looked at her in silence. For a few seconds, Prissy held out the wriggling hamster and then, with a sigh, put them back in her bag.

Eventually Carnegie broke the baffled silence. "Very well," he said, at last. "Paige get the rest of this mess cleared up. I want the schoolteacher's memory erased, I want parents' memories erased and these three children put on the staff rota. And that Vestibule chap can be put back. I think he's safe. Kian, Prissy, Asif, you are hereby recruited into the Secret Library Service as Junior Librarians. I expect your full commitment to the cause . . ."

"I can't do Fridays," Prissy said and did a little jig to explain. "Tap-dancing. Just saying."

Carnegie gave a sigh. "Fine," he said. "Well done agents and welcome to the dangerous world of books!"

Chapter 20

20 - 306.85

CHIPS AND WORK

Mum almost **CRUSHED** me, her hug was so strong. "Where the hell have you been?" she snapped, torn between shaking me and running her fingers through my hair. I felt awful. Mum looked like she'd been crying for ages.

"I didn't know what to think," she said, pacing back and forth. "I saw this weird note from Anthony, and there was all this mess with the books all torn up. I tried to phone your dad but his mobile was dead or switched off." She paused, gave a huge sniff and stared at Anthony. "What's up with him?"

Anthony stood grinning at Mum. I felt another stab of guilt but knew what I had to do. "It's all to do with this, Mum," I said, pulling Mr Vestibule's hypnophone out of my pocket.

"If you look at this picture I took, it'll all make sense." I tapped the screen and held it up. Anthony stared into the screen too.

"What's that?" Mum said. "Oh, that's a lovely pattern, Kian, but . . ." Her eyelids flickered as she fell **DEEPER** under the phone's spell.

"Okay Mum," I said. "When I click my fingers, you will come out of the trance and **FORGET** the last couple of days."

"I will **FORGET** the last couple of days," Mum murmured.

"**FORGET** the past couple of days," Anthony echoed.

"Instead, you will think that we had a normal time, chips for tea, a day at work, all the usual stuff," I said. "We'll tidy up here and all will be forgotten."

"Usual stuff," Mum murmured. "All will be **FORGOTTEN.**"

"Tidy up," Anthony said. "Chips and work."

I glanced around. "And you'll give me an extra couple of quid on my pocket money."

"Extra couple of quid," Anthony muttered.

"Must be joking," Mum said.

I clicked my fingers and Mum and Anthony blinked out of the trance. They looked at each other for a moment and then gave each other a hug. "Better get this mess tidied up," Anthony said, breaking the clinch. "Then we need some tea. I'm **STARVING.**"

"Me too," I said. "Can we get chips from the chippy?"

Mum gave an exasperated hiss. "Don't be daft. We had them **YESTERDAY!** You'll look like a chip at this rate!"

I grinned, though I would've killed for a bag of chips.

YOU DID GIVE THAT HYPNOPHONE BACK, DIDN'T YOU?

*E*nglish with Mr Vestibule isn't so bad, I thought. *Especially since his memory was erased by the SLS, he seems a lot kinder.* I watched Mr Vestibule pace round the class.

"I really want to see the creativity in these book posters you're drawing for me," Mr Vestibule said. "And don't forget, there'll be a prize for the best drawing!"

He reached Prissy's desk and paused. "Good Lord," he said, faintly. "Wh-what book is that, Prissy?"

"*HELL-HOLE HAMSTER MASSACRE,*" Prissy said, making her felt-tip pen squeak on the paper. "Have you got another red pen, Mr Vestibule? This one's worn out."

"I-I'll see what I can find," he said in a haunted voice and backed away slowly.

"I'm doing Harry Potter, sir," Asif said, holding up a tablet.

"Very good, Asif," Mr Vestibule said. "Very good."

Later, me, Prissy and Asif stood in the school yard, waiting for our next lesson. "I think life in school is so much better since we had our little adventure with the SLS," Prissy said.

At that moment, Chapman came **LOLLOPING** across the playground.

"Here we go," Asif muttered. "Not everything has improved."

"Hi, Prissy!" Chapman said, with a huge grin on his face. "I brought you the chocolates you asked for!"

"Oh, nice one, Chapman," Prissy said. "You remember Kian and Asif, don't you?"

"Hi, you two," Chapman said, **SWINGING HIS ARMS** like an embarrassed five-year-old. "It's great to be hanging out with you guys. You're my best mateys."

"Yeah, whatever," Prissy said with her mouth full of chocolate. "You go and moonwalk around the school yard while we eat the chocolates, okay?"

"Okay," Chapman said, beaming and he shuffled off **BACKWARDS**. Being the toughest boy in the year, a lot of his friends thought this must be the coolest thing to do too and joined him.

I frowned at Prissy. "You did give that hypnophone back to

the SLS, didn't you?" I said.

Prissy's eyes widened and she wiped the chocolate from around her mouth. "Of course I did!" she said.

"I think she's fibbing," Asif said. "Do you want me to interrogate her? I was born interrogating people!"

"No you weren't," Prissy said. "You try and interrogate me and I'll break your nose."

"I'm not scared," Asif shouted from the other side of the playground. "I DIED TWICE when I was a baby, you know."

"You'll have to give it back, Prissy, you know that, don't you?" I said.

"Yeah," Prissy said. "Just thought I'd have some fun with it first."

At the end of the school day, Anthony met me at the school gate. "Thought we'd call in at the library, mate," he said.

"Great idea," I said, smiling. "I think I know the book I want to borrow."

The library buzzed with activity. There were kids doing research and homework, a couple of pensioners reading newspapers and a couple more surfing the internet. Small children scrabbled around the picture book section and someone was doing a talk on local history in the reference section.

"I'll have a look in the thrillers," Anthony said. "I love all those spy stories, don't you?" Anthony WINKED and hurried across the library. For a split second, I wondered if the memory erase hadn't worked.

"Don't worry," Paige said, appearing behind me. "He doesn't remember a thing. How are you, Kian Reader?"

"I'm fine thanks," I said. "I keep wondering if Doctor Badd will come back."

"He might," Paige said. "But if he does, we'll be ready for him."

"Yes," I said. "We will."

"I think we may have a few leads on," she mouthed FART. "Might need your help sooner than you think."

"You can rely on me," I said, grinning.

Later in the day, on my way home, I checked out the canal. Dad sat in his usual place. He looked up as I approached. "Hi, son," he said and fist bumped me.

"Hi, Dad, I've got a present for you," I said, pulling something out of my bag.

"What is it?" Dad said.

"A book," I said. "I thought we could look through it together. It's all about fishing."

A huge smile split Dad's face. "I'd really like that, son," he said laying his rod down and standing up to take the book. "I'd like that more than anything."

The End

THE DEWEY DECIMAL SYSTEM – SLS SECRET CODE!

Librarians have a secret code that allows them to organise information and make it easy for you to find. They use a system called the Dewey Decimal System. Each subject is given a Dewey number. There is a Dewey number for each of the chapters. See if you can find what subject has been allocated to each chapter and try to work out why! Don't let this information fall into FART hands, though!

Did you spot the dewey numbers at the start of each chapter?

  000 - Computer science, information, and general works
  001 - Knowledge
  020 - Library and Information Science
  025 - Library operations
  030 - Encyclopaedias
  060 - Organizations and Museums
  100 - Philosophy and psychology
  130 - Paranormal phenomena
  150 - Psychology
  153.1 - Memory and learning

154.7 - Hypnotism

200 - Religion

230 - Christian theology

294.5 - Hinduism

294.6 - Sikhism

297 - Islam

300 - Social sciences

306.85 - Families

320 - Political Science

340 - Law

363.1 - Public safety programs

364 - Criminology

370 - Education

387 - Water, Air and Space Transportation

400 - Language

410 - Linguistics

443 - French dictionaries

475 - Classical Latin grammar

500 - Natural sciences and mathematics

510 - Mathematics

520 - Astronomy, cartography

530 - Physics

540 - Chemistry

550 - Earth sciences

560 - Palaeontology

570 - Life sciences, biology

580 - Plants

590 - Animals

600 - Technology

610 - Medical Sciences and Medicine

636 - Animal Care

641.5 - Cooking, recipes

649 - Parenting

662 - Explosives, fuels technology

690 - Buildings

700 - Arts and recreation

747 - Interior Decoration

792.8 - Dance

796.8 - Karate, Martial Arts

799 - Fishing, Hunting, Shooting

800 - Literature

810 - American or Canadian literature in English

860 - Spanish & Portuguese literature

900 - History and geography

910 - Geography & travel

930 - History of ancient world

LiBRARy FACT FiLE

Imagine a place where you can connect with the ideas and imaginations of some of the world's greatest thinkers! Imagine a place from which you can travel back in time, forward into the future and hop from country to country. Imagine being able to borrow almost any book that has ever been printed. The services that libraries provide allow all of this, but how much do you know about libraries?

The truth about libraries is sometimes stranger than fiction, find out more in this special library fact file.

FAr oFF pLACES

The oldest known library dates back to the Seventh Century BC and was the Library of Ashurbanipal in Nineveh, Assyria. The library was re-discovered by archaeologists who found stone tablets on which history and law had been written, the stone tablets had been carefully arranged.

The Library of Congress in United States of America is the largest library in the world. It has around 128 million items on around 530 miles of bookshelves. That's enough shelves to cover the road from Lands End in Cornwall to John O'Groats in Scotland!

The Long Room library at Trinity College in Dublin, Ireland is the largest single-chamber library in the world and houses more than 200,000 volumes.

Did you know the highest library in the world is on the 60th floor of the JW Marriott Hotel in Shanghai, China and is a massive 230.9 metres from the ground!

Speaking of China, some libraries there have vending machines so that you can borrow books whatever the time, day or night. Some even have special machines which clean the books!

You might wonder why library books need cleaning... What do you use as a bookmark? The following items have been found in returned library books? Yuck!

A rasher of bacon
A squashed jam sandwich
Credit cards
Pressed flowers

Imagine a secret underground library with 52 miles of shelving that contain historic letters from Kings and Queens and other incredible items. The Vatican has a secret library, some parts are open to academics but there are three sections not open to anyone.

One hump or two? Kenya's National Library Service runs a camel mobile library. Each camel carries approximately 400 books and one camel carries a tent so that they can set up libraries to serve nomadic tribes.

Kenya isn't the only place to use animals to help with their libraries. In Colombia, they have a library delivered by donkeys.

The Norwegian Fjords have a floating library on a boat called Epos. It has space for 6,000 books and it serves more than 250 island communities.

FAMOUS FACES

The first librarian was a monk named Anastasias in Rome. He was the chief archivist and took the title Bibliothecarius.

Andrew Carnegie made a fortune through steel. He had learnt a lot through libraries as a child and remembering this, he funded the building of over 2,000 libraries. The first of which was in his birthplace, Dunfermline in Scotland. Some libraries even had living space for the librarian.

Think about this! How would you set about ordering all of the different types of information and knowledge in the world? This mind-bendingly big task is what Melville Louis Kossuth Dewey set out to achieve. He formed a system called the Dewey Decimal Classification system. The system which most libraries still use today. The system relies on numbers depending on the subject of a book.

Do you know your ten Dewey Decimal categories? They make a really useful way to find the information you are looking for in libraries.

000-099 General works
100-199 philosophy and psychology
200-299 religion
300-399 social sciences
400-499 language
500-599 natural sciences and mathematics
600-699 technology
700-799 the arts
800-899 literature and rhetoric

900-999 history, biography and geography

If the book you have in your hand were to be classified - The Spybrarian by the amazing author Jon Mayhew – which number sequence would you look for? Here's a clue, stories and poems are classed as literature.

The science fiction writer Isaac Asimov wrote books in nine of the ten major Dewey Decimal Classification Categories.

Melville Louis Kossuth Dewey was also responsible for helping to create Library Hand a special form of standardised handwriting for librarians to use when writing out catalogue cards. It is not often used any more as most catalogues are now electronic.

Some librarians have also been authors. You might be interested to try books by some of the following all of whom have been children's authors and librarians. What can you find out about the books they wrote?

Lewis Carroll
Beverly Cleary
Theresa Breslin
Madeleine L'Engle
Jacob Grimm

Are you a doodler? Did you know that playwright Joe Orton was sent to jail for defacing library books. He used to paste pictures into them in his local library in Islington, London.

Brilliant Books

If you were to take a guess, what do you think would be the books which are most often stolen from libraries? The answer is the Guinness Book of Records and the Bible.

Have you ever forgotten to take your library book back on time? The record for the most overdue library book is held by Robert Walpole who borrowed a book in 1668. The book was returned a whopping 288 years later!

The National Library of Wales has a book measuring less than 1mm by 1mm, it is Old King Cole and was printed in Scotland by Glennifer Press. The pages are so tiny that a pin is needed to turn them and a magnifying glass to read it!

Sometimes books get banned from libraries. This does not happen often in the UK, but in America people can make challenges against books which they don't feel should be available in the library. Here are a list of some books which have been banned which you might like to read.

Judy Blume	*Blubber*
Robert Cormier	*The Chocolate War*
Alex Gino	*George*
Katherine Paterson	*The Bridge to Terabithia*
Dav Pilkey	*Captain Underpants*
Philip Pullman	*Northern Lights*
J K Rowling	*Harry Potter*
Mildred D Taylor	*Roll of Thunder Hear my Cry*

You might like to think about why they were banned. Did you know there is a special Banned Book Week? This takes place annually in September and is about celebrating the freedom to read. You might like to suggest that your school library or public library arranges a display or promotion.

An autobiography is a book that tells the life story of the person who wrote it. Did you know some libraries allow you to borrow people as living books? You can check out one of the books and they will tell you their story. Perhaps one day you might be a book!

IF YOU LIKE THIS, YOU'LL LOVE . . .

The first book in a new electrifying series
from author of *Sky Thieves*, Dan Walker.

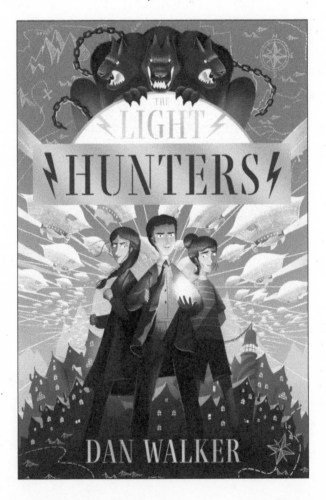

Dare you travel to Inchtinn – where sinister beings
stir and tormented souls seek revenge? What if
survival relies on facing your greatest fears?

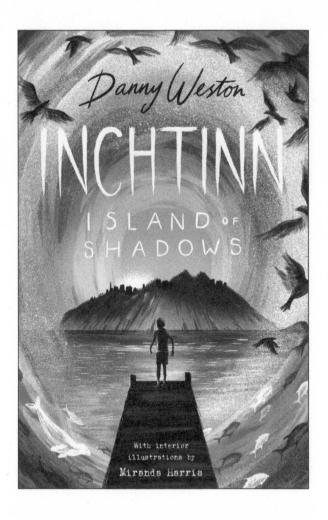

Danny Weston

INCHTINN

ISLAND OF
SHADOWS

With interior
illustrations by
Miranda Harris

The first book in a gripping new fantasy
adventure series from New York Times
bestselling author A. J. Hartley.

"A wonderfully written, delightful story, full of
diverse characters, from a hugely talented author.
Highly welcome and recommended"
Bali Rai

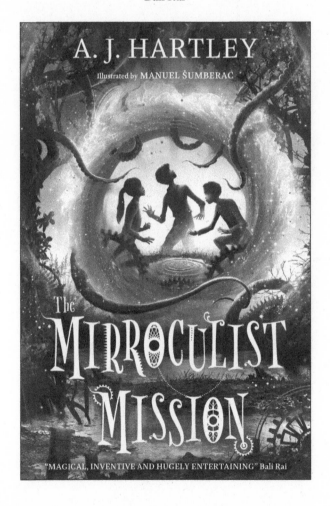

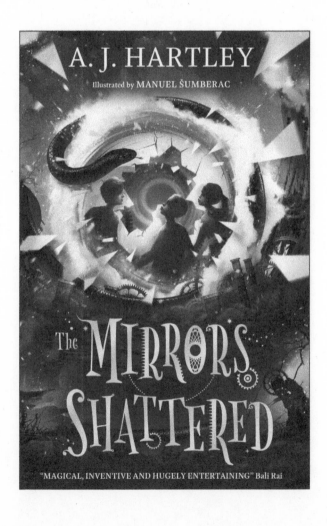

A. J. HARTLEY

Illustrated by MANUEL ŠUMBERAC

The MIRRORS SHATTERED

A rollicking medieval romp where laughter
and action abound in equal measure...
And where danger lurks around every corner.

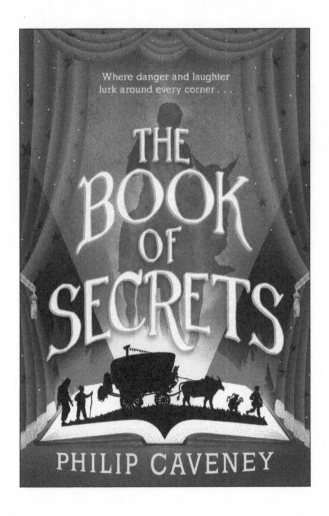

Revamped new edition of the bestselling VAMPIRATES
series, with new exclusive content added!

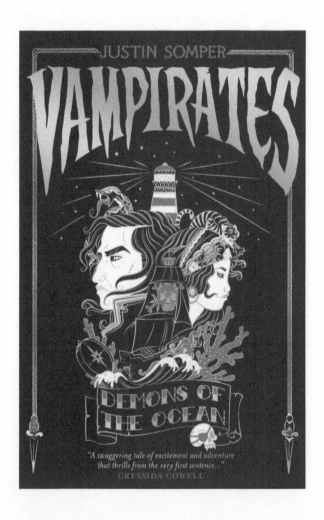

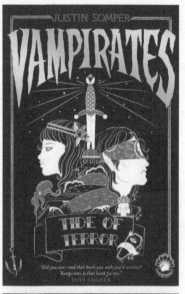

HAVE yOU EVER WONDERED
HOW BOOKS ARE MADE?

UCLan Publishing are based in the North of England and involve BA Publishing and MA Publishing students from the University of Central Lancashire at every stage of the publishing process.

BA Publishing and MA Publishing students are based within our company and work on producing books as part of their course – some of which are selected to be published and printed by UCLan Publishing. Students also gain first-hand experience of negotiating with buyers, conceiving and running innovative high-level events to leverage sales, as well as running content creation business enterprises.

Our approach to business and teaching has been recognised academically and within the publishing industry. We have been awarded Best Newcomer at the Independent Publishing Guild Awards (2019) and a *Times* Higher Education Award for Excellence and Innovation in the Arts(2018).

As our business continues to grow, so too does the experience our students have upon entering UCLan Publishing.

To find out more, please visit
www.uclanpublishing.com/courses/